I0663348

Blown Apart

Blown Apart

M. E. Brinton

Polar Bear & Company
Solon, Maine

To Kay and Frank

Copyright © 2015 by M. E. Brinton. All rights reserved. No part of this book may be reproduced in any form without permission in writing from the author or publisher, except for brief quotations for critical articles and reviews.

First edition 2015
First printing: October 2015

 Polar Bear & Company™ is an imprint of
the Solon Center for Research and Publishing
PO Box 311, Solon, Maine 04979 U.S.A.
207.643.2795, www.polarbearandco.org

Library of Congress Control Number: 2015952512
ISBN: 978-1-882190-17-1

Cover photo and design by Ramona du Houx
Manufactured on acid-free paper in more than one country.

CONTENTS

Preface

Eternity lies within the love a village can keep for its own. I heard this story in its fragments while on my news beat as a reporter for a local paper. I was a feature writer for many years, uncovering yarns to be told. I stopped off at my friend Kay's home to deliver a Christmas present. Visiting with her was her friend Frank who told me what you are about to read—only I have changed names and also re-imagined and in some cases invented what these villagers would say. You have to do this to make a tale.

I first presented this as a screenplay synopsis for my creative writing class at university. "Green light" is what my professor said—go ahead and tell it. I sat on it for the next ten years, and finally while I was out on an island in a cabin, by the fire on a howling windy night, I found the words to write about Dawn and her beloved family and inland Maine life. You see, I had tried to tell a Nazi story through a man's eyes; I had tried too hard to be Fred, and I could not. I had to find Dawn's character and then to picture her—her beauty and woman's point of view, looking on a tumultuous time of history, that being this war, WWII, as it reached out, from within the dreamlike world of a village.

Gertrude Stein wrote, "War is more like a novel than it is like real life, and that is its eternal fascination. It is a thing based on reality but invented, it is a dream made real, all the things that make a novel but not really life."

I wish to thank those who helped me with this project, encouraging me and supporting me over the years to its completion. First to my husband Jonathan and his patience with me, when I left it off for years; I was able to finish it during his recovery from cancer. To Janet, my kinswoman, in whose cabin on that island I was able to write this as she slept. May this peaceful cabin be blessed.

Thank you to my publisher, editor, Paul Cornell du Houx of Polar Bear & Company and those who helped him work with the manuscript. Deep appreciation to his wife Ramona, artist, who read it, designed the cover, offered much advice, and wined and dined my husband and me beside their stream in Solon. A magical relationship we four hold.

Thank you to Wes McNair, poet and author, who found me a reader for the manuscript—who is Elizabeth Cooke, author. Thank you to her, for she gave me such encouragement. To Lee Sharkey, whose course, Women's Studies at University of Maine at Farmington, inspired me to write my stories from my heart—a woman's perspective. To Don Snyder, author, who along with the participants in his creative writing class gave me the green light to go on with this story. To Henry Braun, poet, and his wife Joan, artist, who read this and gave me such a push to keep at it. May the memory of Henry be with us.

Farmington, Maine   M.E.B.
August 2015

Spring 1941 —

My cousin, Fred, and I walked under a tree from which two hawks flew. I shivered, as if a cold hand touched my arm. I didn't know whose grasp it was or the reason it held me back. I remember asking Fred what he was thinking. Did he feel this?

Maple trees lined the streets of this village, and birds took shelter in them. Fred stopped as my heart froze, and watched these hawks. They battled the west wind from the mountains, flapping hard against its force. The wind drove them towards the sea.

He said it was a sign that he must leave for the coast. He was following their direction.

From what are you escaping? I wondered, not daring to ask him. Fred is my older cousin. I am sixteen.

Gray clouds passed these hawks. Bare branches tried clawing them. The birds rose, untangled, gained strength, returned west, over the white saltbox houses on Main Street—back to the hills.

"They're gone," he said, fixing me with a look, which I could not interpret. Why was he worried? What reasoning did his voice hold in its tight tone of fear? "Gone," he repeated.

Was I supposed to comment or continue on the street, past the courthouse? Its bell tower chimed three. We went up hill, past the familiar white clapboard homes I knew and to our grandmother's. A horse neighed in a yard. I threw the apple in my pocket. Dust, blown by wind twists, followed the apple. Brown leaves from last year swirled in rings around this dust.

When I look back on this now, I realize that was the last walk together of our youth. First, it was the last we saw Gram because she had a heart attack that night, and then second, had I been able to see the sea, I'd have seen the tide pulling out. There'd be storms meeting that fleeing tide.

Fred left inland Maine, headed for the sea. I received a postcard from him, saying,

Dear Cousin Dawn,

I took the train without telling anyone, knowing none of you wanted me to go. From the coast, I took the ferry to a remote island. I am safe here. I'll let you know more when I'm settled. Please visit my mother.

Love,
Cousin Fred

I went to visit his mother; knocked on his parents' door. Someone had brushed barn mud from the steps. It lay in cakes on the walk. A curtain moved behind the window, and a little cousin's face appeared. I heard her screech, then the door opened.

I looked up into gray eyes, which seemed to scrutinize me first before any familial recognition gleamed in them. They belonged to Fred's father. His mother rushed past her husband to pull me inside.

"Do you know what happened? The neighbor's house where the Nazis lived—was blown up," she gestured towards the valley. "Fred was there. Did he tell you?"

I shook my head. Not until after the war did the bombing detach itself in my mind, so that I was able to review each ensuing event. The village conspired to take matters into its own hands. Bomb the house, destroy the immigrants' ability to live in our town. The government must not have believed Nazis lived there. The village did. People may ask now, were they Nazis or Nazi sympathizers? Yet, they were foreigners, and their house was gone. Simply done.

"Fred will be arrested. Sure, he will, if they think he did the bombing," Aunt said, as I stood in their home.

The old house shook with winds, but it was warm in the kitchen with its low ceilings. This is a Cape Cod home built by a settler who came from the Cape long ago. The kitchen has a woodstove, long table. Small windows to keep in the heat. I recall looking out to what I love—the endless mountain ridges to the north. The barn is attached to the house. The cows stand close to its walls, out of the winds.

My eyes felt hidden; lids closed over them. The door rattled against the chain as my uncle bolted it. Aunt, weeping, pulled at her hair. Her eyes became larger than her husband's hard ones. My cousin Sarah stood waist high beside me. I remember thinking, I can smile for her. Someone needs to look less dismal.

I made a face, rolled my eyes, as if to say, "Whatever will your brother do next?" Sarah giggled. Astonishing, I thought, how making light of something like that does wonders for the spirits. My aunt took a deep breath into her sagging chest.

She took me aside saying, "Sunlight entered with you."

In a flash, I replied, "I'll live here with you, ma'am." I put my arms around Sarah.

Since Gram died, I'd be needing a new place to stay, but I didn't say that to them; figured they'd realize that.

"I'll be a help to you, do Fred's chores. You'll let me?" What else could I say to convince my Aunt. I could see her calculating one more in the family for feeding.

No one spoke. I remember they finally placed a shawl around my shoulders, took my bag and led me to the kitchen table. They placed a soup bowl in front of me.

I heard Uncle say fence rails were tottering. Who would fix them with Fred gone? I could fix them: I fence Fred out—in a different field. Glare at him from a distance with these dark eyes. Comfort his mother, then fence in our women woes. Let the troubles out to wider pastures.

Sure, I was strong to lift real fence rails, but they'd find someone to do the physical labor.

I sat back in my chair, reflecting on this dinner talk; I needed a sense of how this family ran its business from the inside. I often had visited here, but it was different coming to live with them. I told them Fred wrote me a postcard. They murmured things about Fred being on an island. They could have spoken of a remote planet. You see, in those days, when you lived inland as the western foothills, it was farther than the stars to reach an island. At least you see stars. An island could have been fantasy. I knew nothing, up until Fred went to an island, of life off the coast.

Fred's brother, Jeremy, threw boots and coat on the kitchen bench. Carefully moving into the chair, as if he ached, he said, "With Fred gone, I got more cows to milk."

"Wrong. I am here to milk his," I said.

"You acting as hired help?" He grinned.

"I am no hired help. Shut your mouth."

They put a soup bowl for him, and Aunt laid out freshly baked cornbread. Sarah sat beside him; the attention was off me. I wrapped the shawl more tightly over my shoulders and looked out the window. A raw wind blew with showers sweeping the meadow. Cows lay in the mud. I'd have to see they got inside. Not good to have dirt over them. Fred wouldn't like that.

Childhood best friends we were. Secure in this, I was sure Fred would wait for me to grow up, catch up to him in height, and be my closest ally the rest of my life. I had the misfortunes of life hit me early. After my mother died years ago, my father left for the West Coast. I refused to go with him. Yet I missed him because his was the shoulder I cried on. Gram tried to help me, only she cried dreadfully after Mam died.

I leaned over to Jeremy and asked him if he had seen the house explode. He quickly looked at his father.

"I did. It rose up in the air, ten feet—boom."

"Where were you?"

"In the barn—watching from the door."

"Talk more softly. Uncle will hear," I said. Didn't want him hearing.

"The fiddlers kept playing, but the dancers stood still and screamed."

"Was Fred at the dance?"

"Yep, but he went out before that house went up in the air."

That was enough to hear. I leaned away from him, observing the spring shower coming from the mountains. Weather comes in, altering things.

As the family conversed in the kitchen, rain slashed against the windowpane. The cows headed to the barn. They tottered against the fence whose railings barely held them. These railings needed mending. Uncle is right, I thought. Yet I am standing in the field where the fence keeps Fred beyond me. He can look at me but no longer tell me how I am.

Fred's cows trotted into the barn. Cows don't like to hurry. They must be exclaiming their dislike of this belting-down rain. Following them with my eyes, inside to dank darkness, I could hide tears for Mam. For Fred, none came at all. I pondered what I wished to become, alone without him. I could measure inches to shoot up, like yellow birches in wispy heights.

I could cut twenty-four inches off my hair. It is sand-colored like rock flecks. Gets in my way when I bend over the shallows along the riverbanks. The river will be high from the rain, not a good time to find its gold.

I pan for gold there. My hair twists in the current, messing with my hands. "Swim away, silly, and chase your hair downstream," Fred would say. He panned with me. Sifting for this mineral people said could buy a future.

My hair is below my waist. I can't cut it—why, it's a weather vane! I let it loose for the air to waft its seasons. I used to tell Gram: "If wind blows through things, stirs them up, changes come." It is a way of knowing things about me. Times when it is straight, it has nothing to say—and neither do I, except to know the winter will be long, cold, and thinning out its thickness. Straight hair is unresponsive. I am silent in winter. Lack words to say anything, but I read books. Spring brings the needed herbs, sun to make my hair dense, shine. I am warmed then, bursting with ideas and projects for Fred and me to work on.

I wanted Fred to live in this village. We'd find gold, build a farm together. Leaving was never an idea. What sword—like Uncle's hanging in the living room, beyond the kitchen—pierced this tranquil farm landscape? This sword was from my great grandfather's sojourn in the Civil War. I quickly looked away from it. Its edges and stories hurt.

Fred at home: my cousin gave me kinship with someone who understood me. "You're growing too well," he would grin. That helped unfetter the sorrow of Mam gone.

Fred, who vanished like the hawks—as if neither he nor the birds had any business being with us. I might have stopped him, quizzed him on his plans for spring. These were regrets; they left me no peace.

☙ ☙

The nurses bring me water; the night shift arrives. I lift an arm, looking at it as if it is not belonging to me: wrinkled, leathery, with purple blue bulging veins. I think I sigh, but the staff doesn't ask me what makes me sad. At this time of night, words get confused. "Rest, old gal, recall these stories," I tell myself. "Stare out the dark window; you are not vacant in your little head. You can remember this life clearly . . . Sure, I do."

I thrash around with vivid memories returning. A nurse gives me an extra sleeping pill; I saw that coming. I spit it into the wastebasket when she leaves.

Wish I could tell her come, be part of this past. I am young; do you believe I was beautiful? Chestnut hair curled to my ankles. Walking into morning. Come smell the grass. Put your feet into the river water with me. I even see my mother once more.

☙ ☙

I went through the woodshed linked to my aunt's kitchen by a narrow door, and from there I trudged into the barn, ducking through the stirred-up dust. The barn connected to the farmhouse, so you could access it in all weather. Spiders and dust came into the house; skunks found ways to come in and sleep in closets at night.

I carefully tucked my hair into Fred's old tweed hat he'd left hanging on the wall. Despite this, my hair would spill out. Mam would shake her head and say that I must not have spiders dropping on my hair. They will stay in it, for it is thick like heavy grass wet by rains. I can barely brush it.

My job of milking cows before breakfast brings me to early morning. If I groaned about waking, I only had to think of the cows waiting; I got up. Then, after that, I fed the kitchen wood stove. Foot-long slabs started a fire in no time. After this, I cooked porridge and brewed the coffee. Since the Depression, our coffee was mixed with chicory. "Southern-like," folks said. No one thought it would last after the Depression, but it did. A substance and flavor would stay in the north for a long time. Sharp, root-like, which caught on, and people liked. It was cheaper to buy than regular coffee.

Milking a cow is mesmerizing. You watch cows flick their tails, and flies buzz on sticky tapes. Cobwebs move from wooden rafters. Rusty shadows pry into where light tips on long, worn shovels.

I found a trick to keeping myself at peace with this kind of work. I sit back on the stool, give my hands rest from milking, dream a bit; trick is, lean against their belly, be inside the cow's mind, imagining their meadows; then you don't get ornery and grungy feeling from staring at their udders and the manure and straw.

As I supported my head on the cow's side, I felt my anger rise ten feet with that Nazi house. My anger could have been a hundred feet higher, but by some reports of the dynamiting, the house did only rise ten feet.

That is how high then I feel in my emotions. I can brood over Fred in this barn—churn over his lack of courage.

Or, I asked myself, was it the reverse—he had the courage to flee?

The cows shifted, moaned. An underworld of deep smells tried to choke me. Their movements made a cat jump. I reached for a broom to knock a spider from landing on me. After I stirred it all up, milk, dust, anger, after putting the milking equipment away, the dust always settled back in the barn. Things went back to how they were. You can never clear out a certain kind of grime.

Thus I was on that milking stool, peering through the barn window at the near morning forest. I was swift at milking. The velvety tits crushed as I pulled down on them. It was smooth skin, so delicately thin, that I feared my nails might pierce it, but then, the cows tell you when to stop milking. Turn heads to your shoulder. Sometimes they shoved me because I didn't pull hard enough to get their milk down, for they want to be milked out. It is a heavy weight for them to carry bags of milk.

As I milked them, the soft squirt of the liquid rhythmically landing in the pail, the beasts drooled. The slurp dripped from their mouths, and the smell of it is something you never can forget. The sweet grain, mixed with hay and saliva—how could Fred leave this?

On that kind of day, when I reflected on my job, sunlight barely moved in the barn of this early morning.

Ꮳ   ᏍᏴ

The ruins of the bombed house lay in charred timbers while smoke continued to rise from the remains. It was down in the valley from my uncle's farm. It would become an honored relic in the village, one which you walked around, trying to piece together its past repeatedly. I knew Fred's supposed connection to it, yet it took time for me to digest this kind of violence. The dynamiting—it was told in hushed tones in the village.

News back then was deliberate. There was a large effort to keep it local, and no one wished it revealed further than our village, particularly those who saw it happen or heard the loud explosion. Yes, Fred had fled rather than remain to answer questions about it.

I knew Fred thought of us back home. His presence like a fleeting smile, hung around the farm. And no wind was in the barn—only a still air that weaves with your hair and soul. This foreboding is in place of a sudden departure.

So are the barn cobwebs always there. They reminded me to brush aside loose sad threads. I watched the webs too much, as the milk bucket filled up. My hair broke out of the confines of Fred's hat.

If I mention this hair of mine it is because its memory is so strong. You want to remember a detail of something lovely about your youth. It is fine to hold your head a little high remembering, yes, I was beautiful. No one told me such back then. Beauty is hard to have. You hide it because it could get you in trouble, people said. It was as if I were fey. A cloud of chestnut hair walking down the hill.

My aunt was church religious. She said about self-praise: "Let another praise you and not your own self. A stranger and not your own lips." It came from her Good Book, she said.

I understand it now. Back then, the only strangers in our village, when I was sixteen, had met with confusion. Terror.

"Don't talk to strangers," Mam would say. How could you then trust a stranger's opinion of you?

The young men back then—all mostly hard-working and honest, never seeing beyond their cow patch—oh no, young men were not used to giving praises to young ladies. Aunt usually frowned at me.

Now, an old lady's hair gets fine like threads. The hairdresser comes often enough to trim our hair, put it up nicely for us old gals. I am done with all this, glad to have had a carefree time long ago, of not caring about my looks. But hair was worrisome unless you cut it. And I eventually did, oh my yes.

Ꮛ   Ꮛ

Gram often looked after us cousins in her house. I had a fleece to hold and wrap around me, especially in winter, when I was cold. Snow came and banked up against our homes, as if it would never leave us. We had small Christmas trees inside our homes. Such large ones were alive outside our doors. Mam and her neighbors never saw the point of bringing the forest inside. We had decorations, of course, from the woods—red bird-berries, ivy, trailing vines. We had to get these in early, before Thanksgiving, because the ground froze solid, and snows soon followed. Upstairs was ice cold, always. The sheep's fleece made a lot of sense.

As a three-year-old in the crib, I loved that fleece. I could think back to when I couldn't remember it and stories were told of how I wouldn't sleep unless I had it. Even in a cradle, Gram would tell me that I slept on an old fleece instead of a sheet. Fred did also, and because of these memories now, I sleep on a sheep to this day.

My fleece is with me right now in my bed, just as it was back then. I showed it to my nurse, telling her I have always slept on fleece, since a baby. I couldn't tell what she thought. Her expression became stoic, and she held her breath. Another old eccentric woman, I presumed she was thinking.

"Linen is for ladies," Mam said. She never could agree with Gram introducing me to the smell and feel of the sheep's own wool. Yet, knowing it made me sleep at night, she acquiesced, but I am sure she hoped I'd grow out of this love for the smell of sheep.

Memory of Mam stayed with me a long while after she died. Pa left me with Gram; he went west to California. At this time I sure was unsettled, but Gram understood me. She said, let the young filly tear about its field, do what I like. Gram didn't mind, long as I kept in school and ate her meals. I spent every moment I could outside. Night came with me observing the stars. Blanket around me. "Whatever you do, sleep in your bed at night," she said.

With Mam on the night clouds, I couldn't sleep; I tried hard to pass into her mind, as if she were the wind. I heard her say to me at night, "Sleep, child. I am near." I held onto my fleece.

A sheep's fleece under me felt like I had slept outside. Birds perched on me; flowers grew under me. It is finding your way with grieving. Mam, in Heaven, was waiting for the birds singing in the morning.

Pa said he'd come back for me, even find me a new mother. When he said it that way, or any way—a "new mother"—I shrank from him. How could that be, when you have only one mother who looks down on you? It wasn't going to happen that way, and I whispered before he left, "No, Pa. Don't come back."

A long while later, he wrote from California, saying a war was probably coming, and he was going to see if he could get to Europe, traveling across country on the train, then taking a flight over, and, oh, bad news: he hadn't found a new Mam.

Since his leaving, I had learned to help Gram at household chores, and I was lucky to transition after her passing—into my Aunt's family. With Fred gone, I even had his bed and sheepskins. I had to stop fretting over Fred, and milk these cows.

ଓ   ଅ

I got off the milking stool, broom in hand, and brushed the cobwebs from a window to let light. The sky tells you how a day will go; you observe it, listen to it; especially with spring everything has noise. Dawn is a cacophony of tones. Mam pointed to daybreak. The trees beyond the fields, lit with red, glowed, and the mountain ridges reflected the eastern light. Sunrise came directly inland from the sea.

When Mam let her hair out of her nightcap, it cascaded to the floor, catching this sunlight. "Let's braid it," she called, and I'd come running to help her. As I braided, she asked me what I heard the early morning say. "It's singing music, Mam." That satisfied her enough to hold my hand and look deeply into my eyes.

She called me Dawn from then on. My real name was Zenna. Dawn was the name that stuck.

We stopped talking of sunrise and braided hair, back to the house chaos. It was untidy because the clear sky and freshness of landscape was not inside it. I coughed inside houses; there was little air to breath.

Back then, not much was known about allergies. I suffered from them continually. I had to be outdoors to fill my lungs. At daybreak I could see through the windows the light-filled darkness. The colors were enough to paint a life of pictures. She showed me her books, filled with pictures of magical landscapes that I hadn't known existed.

"That's Italy," she showed me in a picture-book. An artist had painted a golden dawn.

"What country has a red dawn?" I asked her. It was an entertaining game of our imagination. She considered before answering; red would be Turkey, and that astounded me. I had no conception of a country named for turkeys, which spread across the field by our house, when you came out the front door at 5 a.m.

According to Mam, purple was a French dawn, and blue represented England; orange could be Spain. Every color had a country, when dawn came. You had to see such habitual occurrences in different ways to appreciate a rural landscape, Mam said.

She was "from away," not from these parts of New England. Her parents were both professors who had traveled extensively with her on vacations. These trips to different countries expanded her mind, she said, and accounted for her pleasure in studying books.

She examined philosophers' ideas on the subject of the universe. "The universe consists of myriad ideas in your head. Someday, you'll find a thought in the universe to match what you are searching for and that will be when you, Dawn, will find your life! It is a way of saying that life finds you as much as you find it."

ෆ ෂ

It is another night, and I am motionless here in my nursing home bed; yet, from another perspective, what I want to write about are mostly ramblings, wanderings of my thought process now. I remember being sure that if Mam had been alive, she would have articulated strong words about World War II in Europe—as she did on the war of 1914–18—that wars devastate the invisible realm. When wars ensue, the world has to set a curtain across the window on the universe; the world is sorting itself out. Until it does, the universe won't be shining in the window with its powerful ideas and thoughts. Mam drew an analogy of stormy days, when dawn couldn't come with its colorful garment and stories of countries.

ෆ ෂ

I liked to take the pail, empty it, then quietly sit beside the next cow, squeezing the tits and listening to the snapping of milk into the bucket. The deeper the milk accumulated in the pail, the quieter the sound of the milk. The cow might move; the careful rhythm of using two hands to pull down the milk might bother the beast. I was careful, kept on at this job.

Before I finished milking, I had to make sure the binoculars still hung behind the door, hidden from sight, where the family could grab them if aircraft needed identifying. If low-flying planes came over, we were supposed to watch them, write down the numbers on the underside of them. We made notes on where we surmised they might land.

Binoculars were part of everyday life, hanging in kitchens or barns, some of them never used and dust-covered, but with notebooks beside them. I felt certain these binoculars were part of why the universe clouded over; we lived in fear. The newspapers didn't help. They were full of news about Germany. America was trying to keep out of the war.

How did Mam see it, I wondered. Could she see? Surely she is not dead, if kind people shook their heads at my questions. Mam is alive out there in the universe, although, yes, dead in her body, buried in the family grave by our home. A soul soars over the valley much like the airplanes. Her soul waited to listen to the end of day and the birds at dusk. Yet, I could sense, she was careful, out there in the stars, not to come close. The aircraft, people with binoculars—you never know how near the Infinite is.

I hauled the bucket to the kitchen, poured it into a deep pan and heated it to its boiling point on Aunt's stove. Then, as the family still slept, I read one of Mam's books from Rome and waited for the milk to cool to the exact temperature. I then ladled it into glass jars. Some of it would go to make cream, which I will see to later on in the day, when the cream rises to the top of the jars. I will make butter from this, by putting the cream into jars and shaking each one.

The thought of those daily chores makes me wonder how I did it when I wasn't liking work. I would rather read, learn the ideas that shook Mam with excitement. "New ones, fresh each day, are waiting for us, Dawn!"

They say old ladies often speak about their mothers, so I will take full liberty to dwell on mine. She is certainly worth talking about. Such a short life, but my, what inspiration she gave me for my entire life!

Now can anyone tell me what universal principal or being of "destiny," as she called life, intended that she die? It would never be clear to me.

And how did Mam die?—She was riding a horse, pulling an old cart—we were rural, so we used old methods. We had an old car in the shed for going to town, and Pa used it for his work. She was riding in a hurry, carrying tools across the valley to another farm. The horse bolted, went off the road, and she fell down the hill, breaking her neck. Pa cried with me and soon left. He couldn't bear the weight of this grief. He couldn't stand my grief, either. He gave me the door key, told me to keep it under the front doormat. I could have the house, or maybe he'd return someday. I reflected later, his entire spirit had been crushed by her death.

I was afraid right after Mam passed that he was never going to rise from his fireplace chair. He sat smoking his pipe. Then he saw a sign pinned up in our village store: FREE LAND, GO WEST. He told me the sign cleared his head, and he saw there was something to do. Sure, he'd be on his way west. Better than staring at the walls of a room, wishing my mam were back.

The old noisy country bus picked him up at the store. He carried two leather bags. He waved goodbye, plainly thinking I'd eventually come west to find him, but I had to forget that he said he would find a new Mam.

☙ ❧

Each day on Uncle's farm, after laying out the breakfast table, the mugs for coffee, the bowls for porridge, I could first eat my own breakfast and then make sure I rang the old bell in the hall for the family to come down. I washed my bowl, stood up straight, ready for my own day. I waited on the family as if they were strangers. I knew my job. I waited until they'd breakfasted, then cleaned up for them, and retreated to my own space.

In my room, I flopped on the bed to stare at the ceiling or out the window or measure myself with a thin book on my head. I stood five feet five inches, still growing. While some women measured their waists, I counted my vertical inches. If I stretched enough, I would be a few more over the next two years. To wish for that stretch of length, hoping I could influence my growth, I extended both hands above my head, curved my body downward. Then drawing up to my height, I reached to the floor again. Each day began with these exercises. Keeping active helped dispel my melancholy.

You can't grow well with sadness. Never at any time of life. A young person can sink into despondency. Maybe smoke, drink, or in this modern age it is drugs and self-destruction. An old person hunches over. Lungs can't breathe right. Spirit can't sing. Illness follows.

CB   CR

I threw my shawl over my shoulders, took a basket, walked to the store to purchase flour for bread and cakes, tea imported from England, coffee, and eggs. The family lost the chickens to a fox, and no one has bothered getting more hens. I added eggs to my shopping list. I had to pick up a newspaper, too. The world, everyone was saying, is exploding. Times are rough. Rations beginning—both local and non-local economy flounders. People are saying leave the farms. The work is hard. That was Fred for you.

Usually it was quiet in the store. Few people went shopping early. The hired farmhands and I were the only ones who set up our day early, to purchase groceries before they were bought out. Eggs sold fast. They are a cheap food; mixed with cornflour, milk, and baked, they make all sorts of breads and are nice served with soup. The few families that were well off—the village doctor, the lawyer, and summer people—had hired help. If I wanted, I could put on my airs of aloofness, because I was not hired help, but Aunt's helper.

I had my mother's looks, and village people still wiped their eyes when I entered the store, in remembrance of her. Her real name was Adele. Addie, they called her. Addie suited her, as Dawn does me. Nicknames came from the formal names and sometimes fit people better. Mam took nursing training after her traveling days were over. She made a clear point with me that books and ideas are for you to explore as a map of your life. "Dawn, learn a practical craft that your hands can do, and let your mind be free. Maybe you will be an artist, but let the universe find that out for you, while you are helping someone else. It is that easy," she insisted. "Find a good job to do, and then more will come to you."

Young as I was, I understood that my mind and the stars were one, and as stars lit up, so could my ideas, and so I knew not to fear growing up. Mam banished fear to the barn, where I could see it run with cows' dung into the trench. "Fear," she fairly spat the word, "why Dawn, you shovel it out. You may not find a large lump of gold in the river until you are eighty years old. You may live to wait that long to find yourself."

If you look in my socks in my drawer, the ones with no mates, rolled up odd-like, you will see hidden in them gold lumps, size of fists. Don't go stealing them, because they are my cash, and I finance being here in this nursing home with my gold. Look after them carefully when you rummage through my clothes. I have eyes in the back of my head. Back then, mind you, the age I'm at now—how old am I? I forget this— seemed mountains away from what I could see beyond the ridge past my aunt's house.

I didn't need to see over that ridge for a long time. That was *infinity*, my mother said. The last ridge you cannot view. Infinity is where your mind begins, where it is invisible. "We'll walk there together, my Dawn." She said this the day she took the horse and cart out.

That is why I never bothered to go west with Pa. He did not need land. He had it here. My Mam was not the real reason he left. It was for him, to settle something. And yes, it took him time to forget. She took him so far out in the universe, as they talked about it in long conversations. She went so far with him in thought that he was with her; that is how I judged it. He could never come back to the plain earth, daily life, with just anyone else. Because of this, I realized there'd never be another Mam.

I can remember Mam talking with him until sunrise tipped the ridge. They stayed up the night, if they felt like talking about their ideas. Pa said he could not get much from her books on art and such, but talking to her, night ran along the river.

Yet he read a lot; he had his own medical books. He was the village veterinarian. He loved animals, and so did Mam. "Her horse came first before me," he chuckled, pinching my cheek.

I often think about their love. How can love be shared? How could two people, Pa and I, love one person so much? Did love smother Mam? Is that why it had to end? Yet, love looked like it made her radiant as the flowers in her garden. Flowers live just a short while.

I have never forgotten discovering the secret of love. Happiness spreads; golden wings move across oak branches. Sunset settles the day. I see into long ago, how Mam spreads a table of food, and we eat a simple meal, bread, jam, and love.

These night nurses speak softly. They linger by my bed. I like them. I want to ask them if they even know what homemade bread and jam taste like? What will be the things they remember when they are old like me? Their mothers? I almost chuckle here. Certainly not Nazis living in their village.

I skipped to the store. My legs seemed grasshoppers. My height measured an inch higher than last week. And what did I expect to see that day but ordinary business. Morning bustle at the counter, with Mr. B. taking time-out to fill his pipe. Farm girls bent over sweet baskets, glancing at film magazines. Seeing them, I'd dash outside to stand on the bridge beside the store. Wait until the store empties.

That day I slowed down and paused to listen. A crowd was on the porch of the store. They shouted, "We were right about the neighbors being Nazis!"

Up the hill a mile, closed in the quiet household of my aunt and uncle, news was spoken at supper, then hushed until the next day. I thought about it when I milked the cows. I thought about it when I walked to the store. We usually didn't jump to conclusions and never shouted about it on the store porch.

The store was two stories high, an old homelike structure. It felt like home when you entered it, the potbellied stove at the center of the large room. Gathering places, Mam said, like water troughs in a field for cattle. You need to gather to share news.

My uncle's pale face when I'd turned up at his door—they knowing Fred had left and learning that a house was dynamited—was what had turned me quiet. There was a family to tend to, keep up the daily chores. Since we had no answers, we let news straighten out.

Now there seemed fresh plowing of fields. Unsettled mice scrambled out of turf. Foxes jumped on them.

I hesitated about going into the store, past those loud men. I was still in my thoughts from this morning, before the family had risen, thoughts full of Mam; the walk had cheered me.

ભ ઔ

Mam came home exhausted from work as a nurse. After a cup of coffee, she told me her thoughts on experiences of the day—or night—whenever it was she'd had to be on call. "Death isn't meant to be the way it is." When I looked frightened at the conversation, she did not give up talking. "You have to trust me with this, Dawn," she said. "Death is only real if you let it be. We are born out of the stars, out of the invisible; what is spirit but dust lit up in the air, sparkling if we observe it. Listen to the tinkling stars. It is the star children laughing. My Dawn, you always see the stars. If we remember a person after they die, then they haven't died—if our minds have their curtains open to the wide spaces, you see, because the universe, little Dawn, has a great mystery. It is a very small word, an immensely powerful word: love. When you find love on earth, you live forever, Dawn."

I considered this as I tramped the lanes now. Mam, who lived forever, could never die. She was right by me, then. Maybe Pa could not grasp this way of finding a person's spirit stepping with your own.

೮ঽ ঽ೮

Mam's sister, Aunt Grace, was less talkative, more observing of me. She did not philosophize about unknowns, such ideas that grew with Mam and me. Aunt sang in the church choir and made the home comfortable; her weaving loom was set up in the living room. She made rugs and blankets.

I thought coming to live with them would help her spend time making these things. She wouldn't have to make the meals. I relieved her worry over the milking of Fred's cows. No one spoke of when he'd return. I did not wish to hang around at breakfast to hear any speculations voiced.

Before I entered the store, I observed how Mrs. Buford, the store-owner's wife, had taken her chair off the porch and sat in the side-yard with binoculars in her lap, a notebook on the ground, and a pencil stuck in her hair bun.

This part of daily village life pre-World War II had no part in Mam's and my discussions of interesting hobbies in spare time. Mam had binoculars only for bird watching.

She often brought home hurt creatures for Pa to help mend, and birds were some of these, especially young ones in early summer. He worked hard to help them. He and Mam held them in their hands, giving them warmth. Pa said that if we were born with the gift of flying, wouldn't someone be able to mend our wings? He spent long hours together with Mam, nursing the creatures to health. He had no arguments with animals, which is why he preferred his occupation to others.

How could a politician ever sleep, he would wonder aloud, when reading the morning paper. He and Mam lived comfortably, and in the morning, with the news and coffee, the polished wooden table was covered with an oilcloth for breakfast crockery, and in the evenings, for supper, Mam covered the table with lace—"dressing the table," she called it. Besides the clink of coffee mugs, scraping sound of burnt toast, eggs cracked in egg cups, the newspaper crinkled, and the radio crackled. This was a comfortable routine. Each day I knew what to expect, what blend of percolating coffee sounds and smells, drifting to my room under the eaves. At night, the radio played favorite songs, to which Mam and Pa danced. It was a slow, quiet end of day.

Tears come to me when I remember this. Nowhere, not with anyone else, does a home come back out of time. Mam talked to Aunt about Heaven. "Heaven truly comes back," Mam said. "Only Heaven comes in many forms. My home," she sighed, "is my own piece of bliss. Of course," she glanced to the sky, "it is there that we transcend our ideas of home to Heaven." Heaven with a capital H was the place of stars and love.

Aunt Grace retorted that her sister sounded like Swedenborg or a Theosophist, even a Buddhist living in the wrong country, and Mam laughed, saying she could be those and more. "I read many things and take on what I read if I like it, adding spice of my own thinking to it. Don't you agree, Grace, it is fine to do that? Our father never wanted us to limit ourselves. Oh Grace, don't look sad, for I love our steeples and church—it is quite peaceful inside there, where I can think of our parents, who moved on to a better place." Mam did not like to upset Aunt Grace.

"It's because I have to work with many ill and dying patients and give them ideas to pass into. I give them pictures of their memories on earth to die into. This is joyful to them. Part of Heaven is memories of what we have been, Grace."

I sat during these conversations in the sewing room, by its small woodstove, where Mama worked on projects and read.

Memory is heavy; I feel like I am back in these times, for each aspect of it is clear.

I stopped watching Mrs. B. fingering her binoculars, which had taken me back to these remembrances of Mam and bird watching, Pa fixing their wings, our home, the routines we were used to together. Even the remembrance of her talking.

Still, I didn't want to enter that store. I had a feeling that some change could occur for me, listening to this crowd. Fear was creeping like the June bugs here. At night they slap against the windows, attracted to the light of kerosene lamps inside. Therefore, I stepped back from the porch and let myself think again. No change did occur, I think, but still, when you feel that way, you hold back from an experience.

The wind likes to blow blossoms off trees. I think a soul actually likes to blow away at the end. But I need to tell you of this time. It wasn't just war, nor fear. I was holding onto our village life—for Fred to come home.

I knew my village and the farms had to remain. It has to stay for all eternity. That just is. When the structure goes, you'll be out of touch with what is real. Yes, you say everything is different now, of course. But you'll see.

Here I am standing before our village store, apart from people. I don't call it ordinary life, yet it is. The smell of breakfast toast is ordinary, yet the reminiscences of what lies behind the smell are extraordinary to each person. Outside, the river, petals, swallows darting, are of my childhood on our small farm when life was very good.

Outside the store a bird called; lambs rushed through dandelions in the neighboring field. Dust from the road stirred red, and a dog ran through it.

I watched Mrs. B. take those binoculars and hold them to her eyes, check her notebook, placing it on her lap. She saw me and waved, put down the notebook, took up her knitting. She beckoned me to come over.

The running dog loped onto the porch steps and pushing its nose through the crowd, sought food I guess. It made two of us, for I was suddenly hungry and wondered when these people would leave, so I could do the early errands, get back, drink leftover coffee, and chew on breakfast scraps. I knew my place, which was to eat little of their food. I was only one step above the hired hands.

To chat with Mrs. B. was not on my list of what I had to do for the family today. Yet, she might help me understand this commotion. If it's the war, then I had no part of that. Uncle was too old, and his youngest son still in high school. War didn't concern me. It did not occur to me that Fred could be threatened by it.

An old tractor with two front wheels wobbling drove past the store, spurting noise. Mrs. B. and I turned. It was an old tractor, much as my uncle's, and you heard it coming from the distance, like the old bus, which took Fred away. Uncle had to keep his going, doing his own repairs on it, and Fred knew the most of how to fix it. The village will miss Fred, I thought, without wanting to think of him.

"It's the way it is, the turns of life," said Mam, as she washed shirts in her washing machine, which jolted and ground like a tractor. She then put the clothes through the wringer. I helped her and loved the feeling of warm water on my hands, especially in winter. Pa wanted to buy her a new one, coming out in the Sears Roebuck Catalogue. Mam exploded, in the midst of suds. She shook her bun loose, and her long chestnut hair—same color as mine—spilled out. "It'd be like us saying, let's build a new Sears Roebuck home, and ship the parts here, brand-new home. Look at this old house; it works for us; we love it, nothing terribly wrong with it, roof good, maybe a nail needs fixing back into the shingles for next winter—a shutter fell off the barn window in the ice storm, needs repair." Pa settled back in to his kitchen chair. He knit his brow, sighed. He was eyeing Mam as if he'd eat her—rare and wet.

"That so?" he grumbled, lit his pipe, asked her what more needed fixing; he'd get to it.

"Got to tell me, girl, what you see, because I can't have sixty eyes in my head." Pa grinned then and got up, put his arms around her. The floorboards went thump all that night, and I thought he was mending their bed, until I got older and described the nightly noises to Fred.

"Darn, girl, when you hear them thumps and noises, they ain't mending their bed. It's love, and he's loving her, he is."

I didn't understand that creaks of boards meant love, although if I asked Aunt Grace, she would have an explanation an hour long in schoolbook discourse. I did not ask her these things. Fred said I'd learn eventually what I need to know, then learn when to stop learning.

ભ ઍ

Mam said, "When birds fly, watch where they go. They know much more than we of directions."

"What are directions, Mam?"

"Directions are when you have to turn a corner, and you meet a friend you wouldn't have met otherwise. Directions are hurdles, whatever you are feeling. Birds fly for a purpose. They sense the current of air, then fly with it."

"Will I be like that?"

"You'll know which direction to take when the wind is strong. Nothing will stop you from joining it."

The day when Fred decided to leave, when we walked under the tree and hawks flew from it, they set out to the mountains; I knew something was amiss. Fred told me that the birds had changed direction, only I hadn't thought hard about this. After flying to the west, they turned and went east to the sea. At Gram's that night, while I was stacking wood by the stove, he must have told her where he was heading. She shook her head. He kissed her and tugged on my braid, told me to come on and he'd take me to the farm. Pulled the old Plymouth out of Gram's barn, and we headed back to the village. He'd show me milking. Gram stood on the porch with her shawl coiled around her. We didn't know that was the last he would see of Gram. Only she knew she was waving goodbye.

ભ ઍ

I decided to chat with Mrs. B. until all the men left the store. Moreover, if there is anything I hate it is having people around me while I shop. I take time, figure out what I'd like to buy someday, like the ruby necklace from Boston, which has hung in a glass locked case for over a year at the back of the store. Mr. B smiles to himself when I stare at it. I wish his smiling would produce magic and find me a way to get it.

Then I have to decide on a dozen eggs, not pick the first box I come to. Each egg has to be rolled over, to see if there are any cracks. If I bring home to Aunt Grace even just one cracked egg, a look from her would be a mild disgrace. I never wish to risk this. I'd wander upstairs, shut myself in the bedroom and read, with tears falling. I take small instances of detail in a day as pendants about my spirit.

"Mrs. B., why are you out this early with the binoculars?" Maybe it was too early to ask it, because I saw her notebook had no writing in it. She was not bird watching, so close to people. I didn't think she was noting small planes flying low, as we did at the barn.

She acted as if she didn't hear me. Therefore, I stepped back from her, let my eyes wander to the skies with hers.

"There is plenty of time," Mam said, "to find what we have to see."

When you watch a cat before it stalks its prey, it looks around, disinterested, and you observe it until you're bored. Nothing is going to happen. Then, the cat pounces. The passive, relaxed state of the cat is forgotten. It is part of the ploy of captivity.

That was the effect of Fred's letters on me, taking me off, captured, wondering. My rambling, as an old woman, is to lure you into knowing life is always about changes. Then activity, the passive reflection. Pa once said that you don't remember the time you sit reading by the stove as much as when you put on skis and go into the woods. He made wooden skis for me from a barrel, fashioned leather to each side to make a clasp for my feet.

Mrs. B. finally turned to acknowledge I'd spoken to her. She pointed at a high stool on the store porch for me to fetch, which I did and sat down. I tried to look interested in Mrs. B. She was skinnier than half the chair space she used. She filled the other half with knitting yarn, a paper bag with lunch, I guessed, and sometimes the notebook and binoculars. There was a wind-up clock.

The sky was a fluctuating blue, but Mrs. B. had no umbrella on the other side of the seat. "Good morning, Dawn."

"Morning, Mrs. Buford." What was I supposed to say to a lady in her chair at 6 a.m. of a fresh summer day that I must hold most preciously?

She stared at the sky, and I watched the Invisible—clouds coming over to hide even the airplanes. I could feel Mam smiling in that moment. "Binoculars can't examine Heaven," she'd explain. I might appear strange to Mrs. B., if I laughed at that moment of thought.

I was waiting for the store to empty by seven. Mrs. B.'s clock ticked beside me; the wooden stool, even with its height, was low enough for me to put my feet on the ground, hands folded properly on my lap, ready for the sky manifestation of many planes darting across. It felt like church, beside Aunt Grace with white gloves on our hands, dresses ironed, and showing the world our family fared well enough, along the river. The river, which had gold nuggets still in it the size of your fist. I am keeping mine a secret—not only did I pan for gold, but I found a cave where I know there is pure gold.

If Pa knew, he sure didn't go looking, which leads me to think his life had turned, and the weather vane on top of our barn pointed him west—that simple. Mine isn't turning. I was staying. Nevertheless, Fred—his change of direction also came.

"Mrs. B.?" (We called her Mrs. B., usually.) "You think part of the sky will open and let me see where Mama is? Will you lend me those black eyes? Tell me yes—if it will happen."

Mrs. B. jumped as if a car had let out back steam. "Child, you say the most interesting things!"

That was a nice remark to make, only I was not a child. Mrs. B. used to come in once a week to iron for Mam, when I was crawling on the floor. She would look down at me, grin and say to stay well away from the flat-iron.

"Mrs. B., my mam used to tell me to watch for a hole in the sky. You see them circled with colors of the rainbow. They are places where you place your wish and make sure it's good. You can look into the center of the circle and see people you love who have died."

Mrs. B. turned to me, put down her binoculars. "Honey, you're missing the family dreadfully, aren't you, poor child? What else have you to tell me this morning? You talk on; I have all the time in the world. Government paying me to sit here, might as well talk to you while I do."

"Mrs. B., I simply know Mam will come to a sky window for me. She'll pull the curtain aside for a moment, which is all the universe allows." I didn't tell Mrs. B. that if I see a prism, I will make a wish for Fred to be safe.

"Other night, Mrs. B., I saw the valley light up with such a huge flash—did you see it? It clearly wasn't the sky shooting stars out." I decided to ask her if she'd seen the dynamiting, too, which everyone was keeping quiet about, for fear of being arrested, I had decided. I do ironing now for Aunt, and thus I have a kinship with Mrs. B. now.

Mrs. B. was clucking her tongue. It reminded me of a broody hen. She looked up suddenly, grabbing the binoculars, leaned back in her chair until I saw her chin had a mole growing now. I heard a low rumble, thinking it a car, and I started to exclaim about someone coming to the village so early.

"Shush, child!"

I stopped talking. I remember how she shushed me when she listened to our radio as she ironed, with me crawling beneath her. Mam's lace had to be placed on the board, a towel put over it, before the sizzling iron could be applied. The radio hissed, blocking the music. Mrs. B. went to turn it off. She couldn't do three things at once—iron lace, listen to the radio, and talk to me. When Mam came into the room, she fixed the radio; fog made it sputter, that's all. Fog came up the river, up the lane, straight through Mrs. B.'s white picket fence, over the ivy, up to her door, where it stopped. Her door is light blue. Why such a hue? Everything halts at your door if you paint an arresting color. That summer river fog curled fingers into people's gardens, tasting morsels, like a dog half-starved. Flowers were wet, pearled jewels someone had left behind.

How many days since Fred left? What island did he get to? We had talked about when he turned twenty-one, what he'd do. "Speculating" he called it, but "not going west" was his determination, after seeing Pa leave; Fred knew Pa did not find his soul out there. Pa's soul, I could have told Fred, was still lingering with Mam, and of course he knew that. But wasn't it true Pa was getting on with life by starting out fresh as a kid again on another shore?

I must have had eyes that turned swirls of smoke into a burning field. Fred had looked away quickly to the other side of the room, to where the new wallpaper hung, put in for Mam to enjoy. Pa said he'd keep our home for when I needed it. I told Pa that was fine. Mam said waiting was a good thing. Gave you time to spin around 360 degrees and see the ocean while you twirled.

ଔ ଔ

Mrs. B. adjusted her binoculars, got up to walk over to the other side of the yard. I took up her notebook, to draw a few birds for her. I used to watch Pa's favorite bird, the marsh harrier, crest the meadow and dart over the bald eagle. They both landed on a fir tree. People told stories about these birds; they came in from the coast and settled here. We watched them raise their young, let them go—fly further up the river. Young women liked to ask their beaus to tell them about the bald eagles by the bridge. The young bald eagle cast out of his nest had to eventually find a partner and searched up and down the water screeching, swooping over the mountain ridge, until he found another eagle. The village gossips said young women had better tell it to the right man—that he's the bald eagle searching for her, that only she can give him what he needs, and when she does tell that story, he's likely to be blinded. Mam looked at me. "Don't you go telling these stories of bald eagles, child, to any man. You find yourself first, and for God's sake, wait for a long time before you chase a man."

I raised my eyebrows at that. Maybe Mam knew of someone who did that too young in our village. "Follow what you want to do, Dawn. You could be a nurse. You will like studies, once you put your mind to them. I don't want to see you being silly, using your looks for a man. You have so much, darling, but first, find yourself. "I think Mam was the only one who told me I was possibly going to be an "eye catcher," as Aunt termed it.

When she said this mouthful to me, I didn't know she'd be gone so soon. A year after she spoke this, I wrote down what she said: "Seek for your life, and it will find you." Much like the stars at night are ideas, our head has flecks of sparks inside ready to find a kindred star. Sometimes you find the sky is open to reaching into it, as the bird flies up the river to catch the bugs. We see his beautiful pattern of wings, the marking of the underside, and we exclaim in respect for this grace. The bird is simply flying, catching, existing. Someone else sees its beauty. I figure I'll just be about my daily life, catching my living flying from tree to tree and not worrying about how someone else sees what I like to do. I certainly won't be chasing men.

Life can be unexpectedly short, not only for Mam. My friend Nellie walked eight miles every day to help in her aunt's household and made the same walk home again in any season. She never complained; it was a pattern in any season. She had wispy hair, which sparkled when snow fell on it. When she caught typhoid from her cousin, Nellie was gone in three weeks. People missed seeing her slight figure trudging over the long hill each morning and dusk.

ଔ   ଵ

Mrs. B., intent on sky-watching, let me continue sitting on the stool. I wasn't moving, either, as long as the men on the porch argued about war news. Seemed our valley wasn't the same after the house happening. Quietness just wasn't here this morning. A tractor was coming over the hill. What a clamor it made! Some days this is all you heard in the valley, peace interrupted by tractors. Used to be horses. People say, can you imagine a time when people will not know what it's like to not have machines? I look at my hands and know we have as good machines on us, having to use them constantly, so I think that idea is a negative one.

Mam said negativity is like fire spreading. The world is transient. She pointed to the shapes of clouds. "There goes France by; look at its shape! Or there is Hungary or even Germany sweeping by. We can reach to them without the gap of water and air that stops citizens from knowing each other." I wondered how we could get to learn their languages. She replied that we'd figure out a common communication someday. "Look at me looking at you, do we need words?"

I watched her from where I sat on the Sears Roebuck catalogues on the chair at our table. I held my nose from her cigarette. That was contrary to what Mam said was healthy. "Everyone has their virtues and vices," she once said. That was before, of course, anyone knew for a fact smoking was bad for you. It used to be advertised as the way to be sophisticated. And Mam, as rural as she was, loved sophistication. Mam—how many times do I see her face before me? Despite her love of helping people, animals, galloping on her horse, pulling the cart, she needed something at those daily moments to raise her above work. Smoke did it, then. But it is true, as a nurse, she upheld healthy habits. Those long hours she worked took some toll on her, the way I see it now. She loved smoking very long cigarettes. I used to lean back on the books in the chair to look up at the smoke trail to the ceiling. Her conversation took us to Venice, Africa, palaces of the Orient. We walked there together. "Your mind, child, is capable of understanding brand-new theories. That is why I read books, even if I cannot understand them all. My mind is pulled out of itself. Einstein was a friend of your granddad's. Your grandma served home-baked bread for them to have those conversations. She could tell you the law of planetary movement as well as any of those men, because she listened well, as I did as a child."

Mrs. B. said trouble can tear in like coyotes who want the sheep. The Nazis meant trouble. My yes. Government didn't care about our safety on the ground but sure meant to keep the skies above us safe. Didn't she like it that she was paid to watch the planes and to write down the numbers on their bellies in the notebook.

"Whatever for?" I had to find out.

"We are suspicious of foreign airplanes. There's a war across the sea."

I didn't know what to say. War seemed to concern a distant land, not our small village. Although I understood Mrs. B. had this job and had to be informed on the reason for it, I was not interested in foreign lands, unless, like Mam, there was a pleasurable intent behind seeing them. Although she had traveled, I was sure I wouldn't travel. I wanted life to be each detail in front of me, not trying to skim over it.

This led Mam to say you must travel if you can. It is good to uproot yourself now and then. It is like abstract art then—your life. You interpret detail differently, mix new reality with soul. This idea of art, expressionism, became popular in Europe and America since the First World War. Mam felt, however, the war created such a shock for an artist trying to express life that painting what had been before—perhaps realism, or impressionism—hurt too much. I couldn't understand this then—a philosophy of life, which Mam studied to perceive the world dealing with itself through creative expression, but also the destructiveness of war. There I was, Mam dead and another war looming. What would she reflect about this new one coming? Would another art form come out of it? I wasn't going to answer this. If I painted, then my paintings would simply express my peace with my own landscape.

There was proof of her beliefs in poetry and paintings. In each book she showed me how everything had changed. I viewed the colors and forms as best I could, sitting on my chair on winter afternoons, when there was nothing left to do but let the sun sink. Shadows darkened the forest, and the bears came to the fields after dark.

I told Mam, "I love our land here, the little farm, and if I could, it would be the best thing to paint, not worry about the philosophy of what you believe you must paint." Mam said I was wise beyond my years, rumpled my hair.

Mrs. B. clucked her tongue, said I was not listening to her and was daydreaming. "Ever since your mam left, you've been lost to your dreams, child."

She leaned towards me. "Would you like to use my binoculars?"

I shook my head. It was not what I wanted, after all. I'd have liked to see a bird flying, but airplanes were not exciting. There were mountains, fir trees, river bends, which I found more beautiful to watch. There was the day to see, from beginning to end. I gathered the beauty into my dreams at night. Those dreams were not distorted abstractions of my day.

Airplanes would break the silence. They were as bad as the cars, which sounded like rifles firing on dirt roads. You could hear the mufflers of the cars exploding and banging up the valley and over to the next one.

CB   CB

The store emptied of customers. People with newspapers under their arms were sauntering off. I picked up my bag and said goodbye to Mrs. B. One thing for sure, the people leaving didn't buy food, and that made me run, holding my dress, to get in there before the next onslaught, because I sure needed eggs.

I opened the wooden screen door and stood in the entrance part of the store. The storekeeper Mr. B. wiped his forehead with his bandana as the heat of the day arrived. "Why, hello, Dawn. What can I do for you today?"

I explained I needed eggs because Aunt didn't get to the chicken shed yet, and the fox plain cleared the layers out.

"Aha. Sorry about that. Well, on the other hand, we cleared the other foxes out of the village. Sniffed and smoked them, we did. Did you know foxes stink, like terrible?" He leaned his nose into my face as if to put the Fourth of July firecrackers out.

Would he tell me what he meant by "the other foxes"? I stood in front of him, glancing at what was on the counter. Chocolate cookies, newsletter of the village typed up by Mrs. B. I sat on a barrel and watched the cat by the stove. The cat stays hidden while the people talk loudly; then he'll come out to watch for mice.

I asked Mr. B what the crowd had talked about, and he only made a comment. "Only subject is who made the Nazi house rise up in the sky with dynamite. No one will agree whose idea it was, and there was an argument out there before the men went to their day's work. If our government comes in to arrest anyone, no one will know anything about it, we decided. You see, our government did not believe us that we had Nazis living in our village. Therefore, we had to get them out ourselves."

"Was my cousin Fred with them?" I needed to know what the village was saying about Fred.

"Aye, he was. He watched the house lift up in the air, then he ran. We haven't seen him since."

"But, Mr. B, I thought he was dancing. He said he was."

"He did dance. Everyone was dancing at the barn. But he left early because he knew the next-door house would explode. He knew what was going to happen." He leaned close to me again; his nose had a pimple on it, which quivered. "They are saying Fred had the whole idea of doing it, that he organized it, and if the government finds out and wants to pursue this, then Fred will go to jail. Best he stays away. "

I had to sit down on the wooden bench beside the door. The cat curled up there. Receiving information like this can make a person faint. I touched its fur, stroking it cautiously. I didn't wish to make it jump down to hide under the counter.

My heart beat fast. I felt Mam touch my shoulder. As soon as I could get my breath, I had to ask Mr. B. something again. He was talking to the minister, who'd dropped by for a taste of Mrs. B.'s homemade donuts.

"Mr. B. I just need to know for certain. Were the Nazis the men who came every morning to your store for coffee? And I stood beside them so many times?" I'd heard Fred many times exclaiming about them and their German accent.

"Yes, they are the ones. We never could figure what foreigners were doing here."

Hearing this was another blow to me, and I had to lean back. Again, I felt Mam's soft hand on me. "Dawn, you're never too young to learn truth."

I thought of Mam's ideas of abstract painting and that this incident was that kind of a painting. An old home lifted high, as if on wings, flying off. The forms would be angular, not realistically congruent. I whispered to Mam's shadow, "Is this an abstraction, Mam? Our quiet village disjointed."

I remember this moment in which I determined I would have to think older than I was. I didn't usually read the papers. I didn't understand Mrs. B.'s passion for watching for airplanes, what could have been what people feared: Nazi aircraft coming in from the coast and Nova Scotia. I knew our landscape was rugged and was a smart way to enter the country if you were a spy, but I had no idea how in reality it was possible to have two Nazi spies living in our tiny village.

I rushed to the counter, showed Mr. B a short list of groceries; he got them for me, and I stuffed them into my basket.

"Wait, sweetheart, you going to be all right?"

I replied I would make it up the hill and get on with my day.

"Have you heard from Fred?"

"Yes, I have just a note, but I don't know where he is," I replied. I was thinking that my cousin must have left me a detailed letter, and I had to find it. The postcard was too scant. Another one had to be around.

When I finished the morning work, I did find that letter. Seems I took long to figure where it was. Far too long. It was under a milk can no one used. I had thought about all the possible hiding places on my walk up the hill from the store. Fred would put it where only I'd look. He knew his parents would have me live with them—at least for a while. He knew I would be sitting in the barn each morning and afternoon staring at the milk cans, and eventually I'd see the dusty can in the corner.

After I chased the cows to the meadow, washed the breakfast dishes, brushed Sarah's long hair, and my own, I found a place under an apple tree in blossom and opened Fred's envelope. The contents gave me both worry and pleasure to read his handwriting. Oh, beloved cousin.

Dear Cousin Dawn,

I caught the noon ferry out to the island. Please don't tell the village where I am. I will send you more details once I get situated. I didn't give Ma and Pa any details because I'd be worrying them. They don't know I was in contact before I left, with a job offer off the coast. I want to get so far from our Nazis that I do not have to hear talk of them anymore. Figure I will work here for a few years, come home and decide what to do. Please don't tell Pa, but I can't take on the farm. I am done with farming. I will tell him eventually, and then he will decide whom to pass on the farm to. But not me!

Dawn, I love you, always have. Yet you are my cousin, and a step away from that is my confusion over you. I know cousins marry, but it is forbidden in my mind and not safe for children who might be born. The minister told me that. My feelings for you become muddled, because I feel much closer to you than to Lizzie, but I cannot go forward with you, sweet cousin. You are my soul, heart, but our families would never approve. Lizzie and I dance well together at the barn dances. I told her I felt too young yet to be settling down or to marry her, as she wishes this. Cousin, I can't marry anyone yet! How can she think I would be happy? I know we've gone to school together, sat side by side on the benches, but she loves me far too much! I am not ready! And to be a farmer! I feel I would die!

O, cousin, you understand me. I not only have to escape the

guilt of blowing up a house, along with the other men, but her, too! Do you know what life is, feeling one could die each day? I have to get away from Lizzie, until I figure out what I am doing. My friends are all talking marriage and farming. If you settle down, own a farm, you may not get called up for war, that is why. I'm not settling down on account of war. I have to fill life with more than that. Maybe it won't be more, and I'll be disappointed. What is, I won't be a farmer.

My job is going to be caretaker of an island woman's estate. She has enough money to employ many people. I don't know how she gets her money, nobody told me that. Pa would worry about how this could be, but when I saw the job offer, I hopped on it, wrote her and she told me to come. Pa would not like it. I will tell you more when I get situated. At least it will take me away from the village and my part in dynamiting the house of those two strangers, who have been in our village too long. If the police ask the family where I am, they won't know, and you won't tell them, dearest cousin.

Cousin, it is best I am gone for many reasons. You keep yourself well, and dance with the boys. Matt says he likes you, and I am telling you this as a fact. You will marry someday. I am your best friend. If I weren't your cousin, you'd be my wife in a few years, which is how I love you. It is not to be. You will know that is how I feel, now that I am gone. Matt loves you. Please see if you can love him, too.

Love,
Cousin Fred

P.S. I will say it again: I am your best friend—I can never be more. We are as close as two siblings are, kinship makes this so. Our hearts entwine. I think of you with every breath. I will write to you soon. What is better than a brother, or a lover? It is a cousin. Remember this: Matt loves you. Please dance with him.

After reading this letter, I ran down the hill to the store to catch more news of the dynamiting. I wasn't concerned about emotions regarding the letter right now. I tried to put my fear away. Mam said feelings change, and no one knew who'd come out above water.

At the store they were saying the dynamite made window panes in other houses shatter. Government might arrest the men not only for doing the Nazi house but also on charges of destroying others. When I heard that, even though I knew it was speculative talk, nasty gossip, I rose out of my body and then fell down shattered. Good thing Fred left, I guess. Running away can be a habit. You take pieces of the mess you left with you. He'll see it works that way.

I ran to the ruins. Children were playing near it. I went close to the granite foundation. The dirt cellar lay open to the sky; I stepped on the wood, shattered window glass, furniture bits.

What was this bombing? The children and I sat on a rock wall, behind which sheep grazed. Lambs frisked and jumped. A profound calm was in this scene. Only my heart came close to terror.

Mam said to make what you see into an art form. Don't dwell on it for long. Fling the paint, for art is abstract. I had disagreed; I wanted to paint only the rolling hills, farmland, and its never-ending beauty.

Walking around the ruins, I felt dismal, sunken into the cellar, unable to fathom the incongruity of this event. It would take time to piece together. So I said this to myself: When I close my eyes, I see destruction, even if it is only one house, not a bombed city, like what's happening in Europe, the news says. Do you understand, I asked myself, that one house in our village is like an entire city and a complete end to tranquility? Mam, I want to ask you about this. She came to me, held my hand while I cried.

She said that for sure stability will return. "What you see is different from what you perceive. A percept is something you have won over time and is more than a concept. Peace is a concept, fragmentary, only eternal when it anchors in your soul, Dawn. Put destruction behind you, in the forest shadow next to your uncle's farm. I am with you in sunshine."

I lifted my head when I heard her words. These were silent words in my heart.

I went to bed covered by only one cotton blanket, my sheep fleece underneath me. I sent prayers for her rest and for Pa roaming somewhere on the earth, trying to forget his grief and find another Mam. Never. I said a prayer for my aunt, uncle, and cousins. In my diary I wrote, "What is happening to me?" Day was bordering night. Fear into day. Night brought relief, dreams in which Mam held me.

CR   CR

Letters arrived more frequently—another came from Fred. I was curious if Lizzie received his news. Saw her crossing the iron bridge over our river. I asked her if Fred was letting on where he was. She blushed and whispered that he would tell me, his cousin, first. I had his letter in my pocket. I read her parts of it. I will write out the full contents of it here, which I did not show to Lizzie.

Cousin Dawn,

The only thing I hear constantly is the ocean. It carries a roar of high tide and a hiss at low. Tides are new to me, and I sit by the sea when I get time off my work. It is strange to me how the tide can move like this. I watch the seaweed move in and out, and where I am the people gather it for their gardens. I feel very far from you at home. I could be anywhere remote, removed from the world here on this island.

I took this job hoping to escape the commotion in our village of the Nazis and the dynamiting of the house they lived in. In addition, I cannot fit into the tradition of farming, you understand this, Dawn, say you do. I can hear you saying, "Of course." And remember how we ran down the hill to the river to fish, when we two were fed up with things? You also told me how lucky I was to have a mother alive and never to forget that. I want you to tell my ma that I think on her each day and will make her proud of me someday.

When I got here to the island, my employer acted put-out that I didn't get here faster. I explained to her I left fast as I could. Then I laughed, and I guess she didn't like that. If she could have seen the house rising high in the air and hear the talk about these Nazis, then I think she'd understand why I left faster than she thought.

Do people talk about the house being blown up still? Am I accused as being part of it? Are the police coming after me? I tell you and everyone, I saw only the house rising up in the air. My mouth is shut about anything else. Why should the police come after us when they couldn't help us get rid of those Nazis? We had to do it ourselves. I know everyone says that repeatedly. A village has to take its own action.

It's good to be out here. I will never talk and tell who all was involved in that plot. It worked, didn't it? The Nazis are gone, aren't they?

Please keep writing. Your letters sound happy. You have to

address mail to the mainland. My employer's boat collects it once weekly for people on the island.

I will write you more about what I do. I am sitting by the water as I write you this. I am on a wharf. It's quiet out here. I am free from worry and the talk of Germany, and I don't even look at the sky any more for airplanes. Sure, they fly over, but I don't have binoculars to watch them.

Be my good girl and grow tall above the others. I say that meaning in another way. It was a fine last dance with Lizzie, you tell her, night before I left. You can't beat the barn dances in our village. You weren't there, but I want you to go and dance with Matt. He is fond of you. Remember that. I can't be there for you now.

A seal just poked its head out of the water to look at me. I have to get back to what I'm working on, mending the wharf. Got tools, hardware, lumber, and a rowboat to go underneath the wharf at low tide and put new bolts into the beams.

Loving you,
Cousin Fred

Some of this I read to Lizzie. I decided to like her now that Fred was gone. Lizzie loved him, hoping he would make her a husband. I loved him because he was mine, since childhood—mine.

Lizzie said, "I'd best come to the dances even if Fred isn't here. I need to get over being shy."

I said nothing in reply. Lizzie, with both her parents' home and a little brother to look after, has a circle in her life, a magnet, drawing people to her. Not shy, only coy. She is pretty, knows it, according to Aunt who watches the girls.

Lizzie never walks across the meadow to where you can see the mountains and watch the eagle rise above the ridge to its nest, where its young one cries.

Once I told Lizzie I was afraid to dance. "Learn the steps, they are simple," she said. "The fiddles are fast, the banjos lively. The dancers jump, twirl. It's a way to lift your troubles, Dawn." She fixed her eyes on me.

I wasn't troubled. She knew that. People used to whisper about me being strange, when my mam passed away and Pa deserted me. Strange that I wouldn't go west with him, strange that I latched on to my cousin

Fred, and we wandered the valley together always. No—you have to do what you have to do, to part with sorrow, but it is still taking me time.

Lizzie was talking on about the dance. "We arrive in a group; we decide who dances together. You don't need a partner, Dawn."

"Yes, Lizzie, since I don't need a partner, no way I need to attend dances to practice at finding one. Maybe I'll come to watch you dance, that's all."

Lizzie and I went to the next dance. It was dusk. I hid in the shadows beside the barn to watch my friends. I saw Matt, but he did not see me. It didn't look like Lizzie missed Fred; she danced with everyone, including Matt. Matt looked around the room and finally left the dance, walking home alone. I went home after he left, to read another letter from Fred. I took his shirt from his cupboard and put it around me. It seemed that everyone had someone at this moment, and I had no one.

Cousin Dawn,

The sea mist moves like a ghost in the stories we told each other as children. Remember how we imagined him slipping along the river, before the night came. I have never seen fog walk like it does here. It is thirty feet high, striding beside the sea. I sit on the rocks and watch it move. It is maybe figures of forgotten islanders.

I think of you, cousin. Have you danced with Matt yet? He writes me that you look away from him, and he feels you maybe don't realize how he likes you. You aren't like the other girls, he says. You are different, and he likes that. That's what I love in you, my Dawn. I can never marry you, remember. You say you won't marry, but you will. You can't be lonely all your life, missing your mam and pa so much.

I sit writing you whenever I can. I think of you, and then the words come for what I want to say. Sometimes I'm not writing a letter, only notes in my journal, but the words come because you are there, in me, thinking the words. There is plenty to say in my words now. There is no world like this island. From one direction you hear the sea moan, crash, and in the other the wind catches in fir boughs, whistling.

You are not to tell Lizzie this: I am not missing her. I am working too hard to desire her companionship. But you—you would like to help me bolt in the wharf lumber, and I can see you wearing pants rolled up, wading into the low tide or rowing with me across the cove to another wharf.

My employer says I work well. She sets me to fixing all the little wharfs. I work each day at this, and soon, she says, she'll find me land jobs to do. She watches me, and she's trying to decide what my next project will be.

Grasses grow in the moss. I'm sitting in the fog on a rock—so many rocks, Dawn, that I constantly hear the noise of waves. I can hardly see the small lobster boat passing me, about forty feet away. I hear it rumble; it wakes me in the early morning. Comforting sound, like reassurance the day will be fine.

I can write you as a sister, and I am grateful for this. My real sister is young, and my brother reads one paragraph and tosses the letter away. Ma picks them up, and I don't want anyone sharing my thoughts but you. If I wrote Lizzie every day, she'd think I was itching to settle with her, and I wouldn't leave her free, nor myself. She being sixteen. In my mind, too young to decide our lives, but according to Pa, ready for settling into his farm, and to have me take her as wife. No! I'll stay on this island for a long time to avoid that destiny, Dawn. Do you believe in predestination? I don't. We are free to do what we want; our village's minister says angels may have their angelic orders above us in a heaven; I can't refute that because I don't know those facts, but I know we are mighty reckless below them.

Destiny's a big word, but you talk of it a lot and so did your mam. Through you, I have come to believe you can choose your own destiny. You get the feeling in your bones when you have to follow your gut. Not your head; it has to look down at your feet and say, Hey, what is going on? what do you think? So, that is why I can't let Lizzie decide for me.

Before I say goodbye, Dawn, the yellow and purple irises are out, the beach roses smell like lady's perfume, the kind that Lizzie likes to wear and you hate, and the rowan trees are blossoming. These white flowers remind me of your mam, and she was like you, Dawn—light and graceful. Please give my ma hugs for me and tell Pa I'm working well at the current wharf mending. Greetings to my sister and brother.

Affectionately,
Cousin Fred

I think Fred continued his train of thought in the next letter. I sat on the cow stool, as morning came to the barn. I always checked on the other letters underneath a bucket.

Cousin Dawn,

I have this time at night before the fire in old Grumble's cabin to read or write. Forgive me if I send you a string of disjointed notes. I am thinking a lot about home. I close my eyes and see the fields in late spring, the mountains in the distance, and I groan. You idiot, I tell myself for running from that.

Fields, forests, barn, cows, a meadow to build my house in with Lizzie at my side. If I throw that away, what is left? You, Dawn, grinning, with your braids sassy in the wind, saying, "What is left, Freddie, is your life—bingo. Life. Start it."

Wouldn't you be saying that to me? Tell me that you understand me. That is what cradle cousins are for. Grew up together, baby-sat by Gram. There's nothing you don't see. If I tell you I'm not ready to settle down with Lizzie—it feels binding—then you get that. Sometimes cousins marry, but I won't do that. I reckon I love you more than Lizzie, but not in the way Lizzie wants my love. So, here I am away from you both, to settle that in myself.

I miss your mam, too. She always looked at me with those gray-blue eyes, telling me that I had much to make of each day and not to fret about tomorrow. If you build part of your life structure every day, look it over at night, change the angles or pull part of the construction down and start over fresh next morning, then, she said, I'll have an amazing project completed over a short time.

I told her that sounded much like the passage in the Bible about "think not on the morrow . . ." and she said it sounded a lot like Buddha's teaching, too, that you live each day in the present. You quit your worries, because they take you far off in darker places of your mind. Your mam studied all those religions, didn't she? No one has explained why God took her away.

Lizzie wrote me you go to dances occasionally and just watch the dancers. Hey Cousin—you are a lithe, graceful dancer. If you don't want to dance with Matt, tell him. He's like me, more than you think, in that he gets what freedom means, and if you don't want to settle in the village and be someone's wife, he won't press you, and you won't break his heart. He's tough-muscled. His Pa died young, like your mam. At least your pa is alive somewhere!

Now I hope I'm not making you weep about him. I am sorry he never came back, and that I left, but I will be gone for a while, and when I return we will be grown—you and I not just like brother and sister anymore. You will either be married or in a job—or? The future is ours to decide. But enjoy your life, Dawn, and dream!

Love,
Cousin Fred

P.S. Have they found where those two Nazis went? Has our village been under scrutiny by the police? Is my name on the list of those who blew up the house? These are things which worry me. I have no other worries out here, except the d— b— of an employer keeping an eye on me constantly. Making sure the wharves are mended well. No Nazis out here, no politics to follow. An island is a blissful place.

P.S.S. What were these Nazis doing in Maine? If you find out, write me and include it in between the lines crossways on the last page of your letter. Your handwriting is a mess anyway, ha-ha, but you don't know who reads what.

Leaves came out in the river valley. Spring took time this year. I walked up the old road to look again at the remains of the dynamited house. There's something strange every time I see it. To think Fred left because of this bombing.

It's similar to ill fortune coming, like typhoid or scarlet fever. Scarlet fever wiped out my grandmother's family, all but herself and her mother. Her father and siblings all died. Then typhoid nearly crushed our village a while back.

War rages, and we are not used to distrusting people. So, I'm looking for those foxes to wring their necks, skin them, and hang their hides to dry. First, I want to ask them Fred's question: Why they came to our tiny village.

I took my broom, swept the granite doorstep clear of the rubble; I stood on it and thought that I, Dawn, will never let this happen again. I felt powerful, as if I could change the world. Why did we trust two strangers? The truth being, they did nothing to us. They were neighbors, until news came from Europe, and the housekeeper snooped in their rooms. She found letters from Germany, but she said fear took hold of her, and she burned them all.

A rainstorm blew; I sheltered in their shed. Their bicycles were still in place next to old baskets and rope, which I could see belonged to the old days when it was a working farm. The barn is where we hold the dances.

☙ ❧

My curiosity didn't include remains of possessions in a shed. I'd never let a house to strangers. I'd either live in it or let it sit, for its own memories to regurgitate. Sometimes vacant houses fall down when they are left to sit. It only means what went on inside wasn't meant to be digested. Mam discussed the philosophy of houses with me. Even when I was five years old, we made houses out of cardboard on long winter days, when snow blocked us in, and Pa shoveled a path only to have it filled back in. Mam and I cut cardboard with scissors, glued pieces together, made houses we invented. Once, we made a cathedral from a picture of Notre-Dame in Paris.

Pa shook his head at us. He had to go out in the raging storms to reach his clients, the sick horses and cows, sheepdogs, sheep, no matter the weather. If our horse and buggy or the old car couldn't get out, he'd ride the horse or walk, leaving the carriage behind. He carried a small leather satchel with the necessary homeopathic cures. Sometimes I begged to go with him and watch him work. He'd fill bottles with little white pills, scribble instructions for the farmer to follow carefully, then leave thin squares of pink paper for the farmer to portion out the pills into, slip into the animal's mouth by having someone open its jaws. Pa gave enemas and wrapped animals in blankets to sweat out the fever.

"How is it different with people?" I asked Mam this question, because Pa wasn't well-worded to explain anything medicinal. "It simply works," is all I got as an explanation from him, which wasn't enough for me.

Mam said that animals are like people, more so than we realize. Only, in homeopathic medicine, you give slightly less potencies. Animals are extremely sensitive and able to be more quickly cured, because their minds don't interfere with healing as our minds do. She smiled and shook her head. In nursing the medical field was full of enthusiasm for modern advancements in research, public health and the development of antibiotics. She said people would begin to disbelieve that natural medicines including homeopathy worked. She said people would start closing their minds from what once had been healing from plants.

Animals trusted Pa. He rubbed their coats with ginger oil for their nerves, cleaned their mouths with valerian, which also makes them drowsy, and put yarrow into their enemas, which helped their livers cleanse. How did I know this? Mam told me. What Pa did explain, always, was: you have to stay with their pain; they can't understand pain. It is like the world crushing on them. So you sit with them, hold them until they sleep.

"Is it the same with people?" I asked Mam.

"Similar. People can become dependent on you, and this is not the karma of life. You must allow each person free will. The healer must indicate what is needed, then step back. Knowing when to leave the person alone, the family to take over, the art of my work."

She went on, "Your pa travels the county tending to the barn creatures, especially in winter. Have you heard him sing to them? I have see him wrap his arms around a cow, put his head under hers and hold her until her breathing relaxed, and she dropped her calf gently. If your father suffered grief, he'd need kind arms to do the same for him, Dawn. God grant they are yours, or mine, but he'd be like the lone dog, run off to hide."

I forgot these words of my pa, which Mam had spoken years ago. If I'd remembered them when he left after she died, I'd not have let him go west. Did I have any control of that leaving?

CB   CR

The rainstorm ended. I went on with sweeping the doorstep of the foxes, lifted my head to the river wind, sniffing it, wondering if I could divine what Pa was doing today, and wishing I could hold him. Put my head under his, on his heart and grieve with him until he wanted to come home again.

"Little Dawn, come with me," Pa had said on a spring day while holding me on his shoulders. He walked across the meadow to the sheep pasture. My pigtails bounced as wind hit them from the river drafts. Flowers filled the field. I held a grain bag in my hands behind Pa's head. The sheep saw us, rushing from the stream to the fence. Pa had to inspect them, make sure they were well, because they'd be outdoors until late autumn. The lambs ran with them. I counted ten lambs, a good birthing this spring.

Pa took me off his shoulders, leaned over the fence rail, grabbing the thick fleece of one sheep. She struggled until his voice calmed her. He looked at her eyes, teeth, feet. Nothing escaped his eyes. He determined how long a sheep would keep birthing, when it was time to let her rest. He had a separate field for the old ewes. "The happy hunting ground," he called that meadow. I let the lambs nibble my fingers.

Mam rang the bell; Pa put me on his shoulders again. Breakfast was fine in those days: a morning fire in the stove, burning trash, small twigs. Hot cocoa, tea, toast, bacon and eggs. I liked best to sit and listen. I picked at food, as if consuming it hardly mattered. It was the congeniality, the conversations that the meal created. I'd like this part of life to last many years. Even when you are old, you miss the table company.

If you sit at an ancestral table, you hear the conversations of the past. Bend down next to the tabletop, and these stories will come. Someday, I will hear my parents talking as clear dew on grass.

Our house was empty. If Pa wasn't going to return, then I couldn't figure out why I held an anticipatory mood. Hopefully the walls wouldn't fall down. It wasn't like the house where the Nazis had lived. It wasn't going to be blown up in the air, as autumn leaves, its remembrance scattered. Our door was locked.

CR   CR

Mrs. B. diligently wrote airplane lists all day. It used to be only mornings. I sat on the wet grass beside her and asked to see this list. She raised her brows, fumbled with her pencil, erasing a couple figures, adding up a sum, then sticking her pencil behind her ear. Her gray hair held it there as she pointed to planes over our village's airspace. The list had grown.

"In one day, all those?" I asked.

"Yes, child." She showed each written figure. I saw about twenty numbers, and some were repeats and marked with an O. The ones she hadn't seen before were marked X. I asked her what she did with the list.

"Nothing, yet. Think about them. Report them," she supposed. "Give them to my husband to report to the government."

Now that I linked airplanes with the war in Europe, because it was heading the newspapers, I still couldn't make out why we had to worry. I guessed that if Mrs. B. spent this amount of time each day watching for these planes, then she knew it was important. In the past, she used to take groceries around the village in a horse-drawn cart until Mr. B. got her a car. The car kept breaking down in the summer heat or sliding into ditches in winter, mud in spring, so Mrs. B. went back to her horse.

"Nothing beats a horse," she'd say. She hired a farm boy to take over delivering groceries; he has a Ford truck for the job.

"Have you heard from Fred?" she asked me, as we sat together frowning at the sky, like we were predicting rain and thunder rushing from the mountains.

"To think our brows get creased just over airplanes coming across the Atlantic," I replied, adding, "Mrs. B., not to be rude, but now isn't the time to be asking me about him. I expect Fred is being Fred and is fine. I need to know what is going on with these planes, and the village is not itself anymore."

She shook her head. "We aren't going to know that until the government sees my lists and those of others, Dawn. They didn't care about us way up here in Maine—with real Nazis infiltrating in."

There didn't seem much more to say. "Are you sure those men were Nazis—right?" I asked.

She put her fingers to her lips. "Less said the better. They came through our forests down from Canada. Down our road here. Thought it looks like a far-off place to hide. They didn't know we'd discover what they were doing."

Mam discussed the best intentions of each country. She recited German poets at night to Pa and me. He yawned, rocked in his chair, smoked a pipe. Sometimes I thought he was only looking at Mam, her hair let down from the bun, falling like water to her knees. Mam never forced her love of literature on us. I liked the low tone of voice she spoke in. Soothing, Pa used to say. I remembered the sound of the winter winds against the windows at night as she read. Like the beating of rugs, snow thumping off roofs onto ground was Mam's voice reading the German language.

Germany had fine poets and thinkers; she had her shelves filled with books of Goethe. She would be horrified to read the news that Hitler, acting as dictator, was ruining Germany. I was confused what the word "Nazi" meant.

"A German isn't necessarily a Nazi, Mrs. B., right?" I was squishing my eyebrows down to my eyelashes, like turning a lemon in its skin down to its pulp.

"Of course not, child." She tapped the pencil on the chair's armrest.

"Where did those two men go, with their house blown up?"

"Gone from our village, that is for sure. Down to disappear into a city, that's what Mr. B says."

She leaned close to my head. Her hair was damp, as if shaken out from a bush. "Down to Lewiston, child, that's where they're hiding out. Now, don't you go telling anyone I'm the one telling you that! It's what the men at the store are saying, when they come in for their corn and tobacco."

I was thinking that since I had a day off soon, I'd take the bus down to Lewiston and find these men myself, give them a piece of my mind for making Fred run off. Don't expect they'd understand that. And it might put Fred in trouble. I wished to tell them how awful they were to ruin my safe world of having my cousin Fred nearby.

If I were to decide to go to Lewiston, I'd have a lot to plan. I wouldn't tell Fred. I had to find them, so that I could stop this fear in my heart, which kept me from sleeping. "Like the worry over whether your man will be gnawed by a lynx," Aunt used to say to Mam, when she didn't think I was listening. "Not my man!" Mam laughed. He loves the animals; they won't harm him.

"I'd just as soon as a lynx jump on my man," said Aunt, who was frustrated over her husband not seeming as if he loved her anymore, I heard her tell Mam. "And I don't touch him because he jerks when I do."

Mam retorted, "Could be he's very tired, and unhappy. Farming is hard labor. Give him time; he'll come around."

Lynxes roamed our forests, dropping from maple trees, birches, firs, landing on you, if your horse went slowly, slashing their claws into your neck. To even whimsically think of them jumping off a tree onto Uncle made me shiver. I felt sorry for Aunt.

ᶜᵇ   ᶜᵇ

Mist rose from the river; I looked down into the valley. Clover grew in the fields with daisies fringing the dirt lane. I breathed deeply. How could I tell Mam that this beauty was still the same? She used to look on it and dreamily tell me this valley was a treasure on earth—our village. A treasure you can't share with everyone. You put it in your breast before the world is awake and share it with someone you love.

"Nazis walked into it, stole it," I whispered to Mam.

Wind rushed out of the north, shook the elm tree and whipped my long hair around me twice. I took my calf-length curls, twisted them ten times, tucked them under my left arm in a farmer's tether. As suddenly as it had arisen, the wind died.

"I am sharing this beauty with you today, Mam, even if I have troubles now. The knot in my hair held the reins of my anger. I'm going down to old Lewiston, with its sooty mills and drunkards on back streets, to find the Nazis."

I couldn't share this idea with Pa, because he was gone. Did Mama know this up there in Heaven? Did I do the right thing in staying in our village, instead of accompanying him out west? Was he taking care of animals somewhere else, or had he found a new Mam? I remembered my last hug to him and how he beseeched me to come with him, and I said no, that I didn't like travel.

"So, if you couldn't follow him, then don't go chasing strangers, either, Dawn," I clearly heard her say. I stumbled in the field with the river releasing blue light and mist departing.

"Are you the mist, Mam?" I asked her back. I stared into this vapor. The voice of this immeasurable essence spoke to me through the only way I could hear it as Mam's own words. I slipped into the barn, milked the cows, and then put my paper on top a milk bucket and scribbled a letter to Fred. I would tell him that the government was going to be investigating our village's Nazis now, and it was off our shoulders—we are safe, except that Mrs. B. keeps her list of planes. And the Nazis have gone just a pace away, down to Lewiston. Mrs. B. told me not to tell anyone. So don't you, Fred, spread it any further.

I wrote Fred.

Cousin Fred,

No one knows where you are. I keep that quiet, even if it's hard to keep my pencil from telling you what Mrs. B. tells me. She also said because we are rural here, it is a place for German spies, and we have power now—we took it into our hands to kick them off, out of the village, blow up their house, and if any more come, we'll do it again, and the government won't stop us.

Love,
Cousin Dawn

By the end of writing that brief message, I had decided not to take the bus to Lewiston. It'd make a good story to say that I had, but I'm not inventing it that I did. When I heard the voice of Mam in my heart telling me not to, I listened. You have better things than to waste your pay on taking a bus to chase strangers, I told myself, repeating Mam's words. I knew then she sees into my day.

In my diary I said,

Days going into summer from spring. Apple blossoms are gone. Peepers in the swamps are nearly over; one calls out to the others to start up, but a few respond, then stop. Crickets take over from peepers and call all night. Dances are every week. I go to each one, following Fred's advice, but I don't dance. I tightly braid my hair into a long rope down the back of my knees. The rope keeps me tied up, tied firmly.

I wear the same plain gingham dress, ironed with starch. I watch to see if my prim appearance works. I have never wished to be asked to dance.

Those dances were strained affairs. I never liked them. Now, you read all sorts of literature about the history of villages and their dances. I wish I could have a pleasant memory for them. And I don't know how after a hard day of work we all danced. It'd be like telling the nurses here on their feet all day to go home, make supper, then dance. Maybe it'd work. A way to ease anxiety. No one took pills for distress then. Of course, we had our troubles. At the dances, if you went barefoot it hurt you. Blood marked those who kicked off their shoes. Matt watched me from a distance. I had bare feet; I sat on the bench and kept time shuffling them. I shook my head at him.

He wore his cleanest jeans, checkered shirt, and a sad look, as if he were up the barn rafters, looking down. My heart went out to his, because I perceived he was closer to understanding me more than I thought, yet I stayed on the opposite side of the barn. I wasn't ready to forget myself. I loved the music: fiddles, accordion, but that was the limit to my involvement with the dance. Sometimes my feet wanted to swirl my body, and when that happens, you have your feelings and let your mind catch up with your heart.

Mam said we think our mind is the leader, but it's the combination of heart and mind, not the mind alone. "When your heart is lagging behind, stop and listen, Dawn."

Mam knew of an editor who because she went to Columbia University wouldn't read the kind of writing that came from the heart. "Think on that," Mam said. "She's missing poetry and folktales and female writing, softer words. Think how much she avoids."

"She only wants to find a man, make him a famous writer, then marry him," Pa remarked. I laughed when I heard that. Mam replied that this editor ended up marrying late, her childhood friend, a rich boy by birth. I wondered at the kinds of people Mam knew. She went on to say that this editor said no one who lives in Maine can write.

"Sounds like she thinks Mainers have no stories to tell." Pa grinned.

Mam shook her head, as her eyes searched for lights of struggling cars out the window. Cars stuck in the mud.

"Her name is Nina," she said, her mind half in her words now. Wheels were spinning, churning, no clear way out of spring mud season.

Pa swore quietly, only I heard him, "Then, Nina, you'd better f— come up here." He went out to get the rope to pull out the car. Mam followed behind the shining coil.

CB   CR

Where I sat on the bench on the dance floor, there were swallows darting above me into nests on the rafters. Cobwebs slanted down to my head. The spiders caught the black flies. In a barn you let the realm above your head have its own life.

The music rushed upward to the ceiling; I spied gnats doing figure-eight patterns there. "Summer and gnats spin," my Gram had this saying for hot days.

Matt looked at me. If only Lizzie would ask him to dance. That way she'd get over Fred and stop pestering me for news of him. I know he wrote me far more frequently, and I supplied him with news of the daily life at his home. I told him how his brother was slacking off work lately, and his father missed him, and the sister was doing well with summer school and catching up on her math. Aunt liked it that I was good at cheese making.

Something was wrong in this equation, I kept thinking. Life felt good, yet running away from me, as Fred had done—I had no ideas for my future. I missed him, yet I could not have him with me anymore. He had separated his life from mine by going to that island.

I thought my letters dull for Fred; usually I sent him postcards, saying nothing much. He kept most of my letters and cards and gave them back to me when he was older. Here is one.

Cousin Fred,

I walked with your sister to the field yesterday. She is a big help to your ma. She is growing taller. Jeremy works hard, and I see little of him. I don't like the dances. I sit and watch. Matt is kind and asks after you. We send you our best. Everything is well enough here. Your cows give plenty milk. I am quite good at milking now.

Love,
your cousin Dawn

I was cautious not to say anything of importance in postcards, because anyone could read them. For letters to him—since the Nazis had not returned, and the government did not pursue the people who had blown up the house, Fred had no reason to be on the run for some time. Since he loved excitement, I was tempted to tell him a good tale: our village men tracked down and brought to court, still looking for Fred— But alas, I had nothing to write but the simple truth. Maine was so far from Washington, DC that no one paid attention to us. I told him Mrs. B. continued to sit in her chair and send lists of airplanes to the government.

Matt sat next to me. Although shy to dance with him, I felt comfortable with him sitting there on the bench. Why was it when we got older, we began to act differently together, as if we did not know each other anymore? Knowing Matt since grade school, I accompanied Fred and him to the riverbank, where we often fished. Why is he acting as if I'm not Dawn, but someone apart from him, an object? I glanced at my dress. Yes, I was dressed properly. A braid holding back my hair, not letting it shoot off in wildness. I regretted putting it into tight knots, and even wearing a dress. If I'd worn my regular clothes, blouse and trousers, he'd be treating me normally. I must have taken an extra breath and gasped, for he asked me if I needed fresh air. Could we step outside?

I remember replying in the affirmative, and my cheeks were red with heat; I know the girls will gossip afterwards, saying, "They left the barn, of course for the purpose of kissing."

It will be different. I'd see to that. We went to the apple orchard on the left side of the barn, where he pulled out a tobacco pouch, rolled a cigarette and blew smoke into the air. We were silent. It seemed an hour, but finally he turned around and looked at me as if I were a star overhead, and stars do shine and the crickets steady their voices in the dusk.

"I've known you since a child, Dawn. I don't have words right now for you. Because tonight I see you differently, like you are in a gown, going to get up and dance off. All grown, leaving me and our friendship behind, and I don't want you to go. You're beautiful, Dawn, like the slim iris flowers." He pointed to them by the barn door.

I stepped back and held my hands. "You hardly know what you're saying. I'm only Dawn, and I'm not leaving town, going dancing in the future. I have nowhere else to go except up there, where Mam lives"; I pointed to the sky. "Or out there." I pointed west, "Where Pa went." Matt continued to smoke.

I wanted to smoke. "Can you roll me one?"

Everyone was smoking in the village with this war talk hanging over morning news in the store. Even old Mrs. B. in her chair had switched to the long, slim cigarette in a cigarette holder. Mam had loved them. But old Mrs. B.—why, you'd think it was past her days to smoke. "I think better when I smoke, child," she said as she watched the airplanes.

The men went into the store, read the newspaper and smoked, talked longer than their chores. They rushed through the day on account of hearing more news; then they returned to the store after work to smoke again and talk. "Village peace pipes," Mr. B. said, when I stared at him lighting up his second cigarette in a row.

"What are you thinking about?" Matt ground his third cigarette into the grass, until the last ember died.

"I want life normal again." House blows up, Mrs. B. watches the sky, and Fred disappears. I want to talk to Mam all the time these days about my life, and she is gone. Aunt attends church prayer groups every day. She won't answer any questions about Nazis, airplanes, or what she prays about at these group meetings. "Just ask me no questions," she snaps at me.

Matt leaned forward as if to hear me better. I sat down on the grass.

"Remember, you got to talk softly, Dawn, when you say that word, 'Nazi.'"

"I know. To Aunt, a Nazi is a bug, a thing to squish, get out of sight like the way she swats flies. And Mrs. B. said Nazis have nothing more to do with us. She is obsessed over air traffic. As if Martians would gun us down from above."

Matt sighed, saying that he is trying to leave all this alone. He wants to farm, maybe never leave home, unless something else comes up. "No war can take men from our river valley or change our way of life. No foreign land can do that. Can it?"

I had no answer to this. I shook my head.

"Fred is the only one who has left." He stated this as if he couldn't believe the fact.

Then tears came to my eyes, and I didn't mean to be sad. Matt handed his handkerchief to me and waited until I could speak again. His fourth cigarette was a burning coal in his fingers. With his other hand, he held my hand and said not to worry about Fred: he will decide when to come home. Best he's away until the house blowing up with dynamite is finally no more discussed. We have to be certain that the government isn't going to press charges on the men in the village. "If the government was too damn scared of taking the Nazi problem into its hands, even disbelieving us that we had Nazis in our village, then we have a right to get rid of them."

"Yes, Matt. Everyone is saying that. So where are they gone to?" I whispered.

"Someone from the village has been spying on them. I can't say more. The Nazis are heading to New York City on a train. That's fine by me. Let the big city deal with them. Apparently there are areas of Nazi supporters in the cities. Government ain't too worried, either."

I gripped his hand. I had nothing more to say. We listened to the music coming through a slit in the barn door. I hoped my cousin was safe on his island and the village out of danger from the Nazis. Let the city sweep them up. I kept Fred's whereabouts a secret from even Matt. Secrets keep people safe if they are part of a wound. I could hear Mama say that to me.

Fred's wound was healing, maybe, out at sea. Lizzie couldn't see that he had to leave the farm, couldn't settle down until he felt safe. Safe means how you feel with a gun, or how you feel with yourself. Are you walking the river path where you know you can place your feet above spring flood level, or are you stepping where mud will pull you in? Pa would tell me to trust the ground under me. Fred had to feel secure where he was going.

Silver edged moon was above the trees; streaked light through fir branches. Lit up the meadow. He kissed me. I thought to smack him, but my tears were falling instead.

I leaned against him, waiting for my sobbing to quit. Hate it when I can't stop crying. I think how loneliness churns me. With Matt there, that night, as I recall so much of it, how, if I stay near him, warmth can cover the sore. Matt without his pa and I without Mam. Was that it? With my arms about him, friendship deepened as the dark part of night draws the moon to it.

After that, I stopped battling something inside; I let down my hair again, worked hard at the basic chores, and each day after milking, I made perfect butter, cheeses, even cleaned the house. I agreed to help Matt with haying if I had free time.

The first kiss left me awkward, though. Night ended, stars vanished. No sunrise came. "Oh, Mam," I whispered.

I went about my day. Perhaps Fred didn't feel safe, like this, in Lizzie's arms. He wasn't rooted, and he had no need to feel safe in another's embrace. And do I wish to hold someone, as if they are my anchor? I am younger than Fred, so why should I be feeling like settling? I always followed Fred. Maybe I should be running too, but my heart is telling me I am opposite Fred now. I am rooted.

"You have to let go of everything you doubt. Matt comforts you, Dawn." Mam said these words.

Thus, I would follow this new sense of myself as flowers spread in the summer meadow, the fireflies of evening dart. To cherish the look in Matt's eyes when he sees me walking up the ridge to his home.

"You're only home when you feel yourself at home on the earth," Mam said. She lived with brilliant lights flashing, her purple shawl she wore on earth about her.

"Mam, are you warm out there in the universe?" There, life is your own mental picture of cold or warmth, and if you can remember being warm on earth, you take that thought and feel the warmth around you in the universe.

CB   CA

Stood on the river rock—the water rushing and the noise like staccato notes going over the shallows. Should I be striking out from my village to find Fred? I thought the question would not depart from me, yet, holding Matt's hand and the summer in high grass, despair over Fred lessened. I let a stick in my hands dangle, watching a fish swim up to it, then quiver away. The trout were so thick I decided to get my fishing rod and was about to leave, when Matt waded into the river to my rock.

"What are you thinking, yellow cat?" It had been his name for me since I was five and I tagged along with Fred and him. I had yellow hair to my feet then and used it to step on when my bare feet got cold on the kitchen floor. I wouldn't let Mam cut it.

I told him, nothing much, old thoughts returning like, like maybe doing something more than tend my aunt's place and milk Fred's cows.

Matt bent his head down, grabbed my hair in his teeth, and pulled me towards him, and I yelped and put the stick in the river bottom to balance; it wasn't deep there.

"I'm not sure you are ready yet; when you are, let me know because I'll be at your service, sweetheart, to help you find yourself."

"Matt, you'd be a hindrance to me if you did that."

"Then, what are you thinking?" he said.

"Something like buying paints and setting up a place like Mam said I should do. A little place to paint my landscapes."

"You sound more yourself saying that."

I swirled the stick to touch another fish. "I'm sure it's what Mam wishes me to do."

"Then we'll get you set up. We'll show your art in galleries. It doesn't make much sense striking out alone. Let me help you. You'd be disappointed in yourself eventually."

He sounded like a salesman to me. He was making his sales pitch about himself. Well, I had to stop to think, there in that river. I needed somebody, for sure. I also trusted him. I rested my head against his shoulder—maybe shouldn't have done that—hoping he didn't think I wanted his arm around me.

I leaned there, watching the water, the dragonflies. Thought a little more about my painting: a field with shadow and borders of sky, where Mam sleeps. Only what bothered me was, whenever I pictured a landscape with a field, I saw the house where the Nazis had lived rising up out of it.

"We'll fix up your folks' home for your place to paint," Matt said.

"Don't know how to paint the picture I wanted to do."

"You can paint, Dawn, it'll return; you'll remember everything you want to do with your paints. Worry over war is like this, Dawn."

"I remember Mam saying this, too. War divides beauty."

Mam had said, "You have to see the way a spring leaf unfurls. Grows in light. Then later, as a dead leaf, crumbles. Memory coexists with life." She sewed a quilt as she spoke to me in her kitchen.

I thought for a while. We were on the rock still. Water was a good distraction. I needed time to reflect here. Even to have Matt leave me alone.

"Maybe I could bear to go inside her kitchen again." I had let ivy cover the windows. Let mystery fall. Pa had said it was mine whenever I wanted to live there and had paid Uncle a sum to keep it looked after for me.

Matt twined my hair in his hand. "You could find a room in it to start, little waif."

That was another name he called me, when I was skinny. No one looked twice at me, only at my hair. Here was Matt, taking me from my own thoughts, while looking directly in my eyes.

"Not now, Matt."

"One kiss, waif, just one?"

My heart was suddenly heavy. "We need to talk this over, not kiss."

He shrugged, and let go. "We can bring them back only for moments. Other times we have to let them go from us. Pa comes back to me at sunrise, when I'm driving the cows out, and he calls to make sure I get home to Ma and eat breakfast. I see him waving before he disappears, smiling at dawn."

When he said my name, even though he meant the sunrise, he looked at me and a tear formed in his eye, dropping to his cheek.

"We are very young, Matt, to have lost what we love best." I brushed away my own tear. Looking at him there, small tremors went through me, into my fingers, like ripples in water, where I dangled my feet. Matt took my hand; we sat there until the whistle from the feed mill called workers back from lunch and made me jump.

"I have to start the supper for Aunt Grace!" It took me hours to prepare it. I had to cook, cleaning and preparing vegetables, airing the downstairs, shaking rugs while food simmered.

Wistfully, Matt said he'd buy me a box of paints and see me Saturday at my house. It sounded so real, saying it like that, as if Mam would be there for Matt and me. We'd step then through the cobwebs and ivy into her kitchen.

CB   CR

On our way home, we met Lizzie.

"Have you heard from Fred? I was just up to his home asking if he'd written anyone in the family." Wearing a white shirt and plaid skirt, she stepped in front of us, wrinkled her nose, showing annoyance.

"No, it's been a couple weeks with no word from him."

"Well, I'm anxious for his health and his safety. I don't even know where he sleeps or if he has a job." Lizzie tossed her hair.

I didn't want to tell her too much. "Maybe he sleeps under a rowboat at night." I said this with a laugh, which I hoped would cheer her. But this lightness concerning Fred whom she adored produced the opposite effect, and she cried. I held her until the sobs were done, the past was done, the Nazis done, and holding her felt as if we had bonded in this despair that wracked us, only now because of it I had a dear friend, Matt, who let me touch his tears.

Although Lizzie had her parents and younger siblings, there was no one close as Fred had been to her, to listen to her thoughts and fears.

"Lizzie, living is letting someone have total freedom. Let them even mess up and die." She bothered me. This is how I let Pa go.

"Mam read me myths," I told her, "where fear of unknown places could stop people from venturing into new territories; if they managed to keep on going, they might find the next adventure. Through dark times, this courage to keep on is an example for other people."

Lizzie wiped her tears. Those days had winds blowing autumn ahead of itself. Matt waited until we caught up to him.

"What is your adventure then, Dawn, do you have one?" Lizzie asked.

"For sure; it isn't going to be running around the world without a plan in mind. Matt is helping me set up a painting place, in my old home, where I can do what Mam and I talked about—painting and making abstractions; I can't yet abstract an idea on paper into a painting. Matt says I need courage to paint what I like. That is my adventure, Lizzie. I have no energy to run off, especially as Matt is coming close to me and I to him, and he has his farm to look after."

Lizzie watched the bus pull up to the store. It coughed, choked and let out a bang. Usually that made us laugh and run fast to see it pull off to Augusta or Lewiston. Today we stared at it and the people boarding it. I was still thinking of the two Nazis. Now Mr. B. scrutinized each person to know who got on or off that bus. If he didn't know them, he asked what were their plans of visiting our village. If I were to board the bus for Lewiston, as I thought the other week, to find these men, he'd have told Aunt as fast as lightning hit cows in the field.

Lizzie said, "Someone needs to check on Fred, find him, make sure he is fine." She had such a piercing light in her eye that I quickly assured her that Aunt and Uncle know he is well, only they aren't telling everyone. I didn't let on I had letters. I wasn't going to have her boarding the bus to find him. Her Ma would be done for, if Lizzie were so selfish and left like that.

"Lizzie, one thing for sure, you are not to try to find him yourself." I told her so. I can get cross with my friends. Lizzie will think about these words and know they are true.

In the store, Mr. B. greeted us, raising one of his brows. He then walked to the mail cubbyhole and brought me a letter. Weathered, it was yet intact; Lizzie went red and clasped her hands together. We went out to sit on old butter churns. Matt waved goodbye to me and continued up the hill.

Lizzie's youngest brother came running round the corner of the store, stirring up dust, his cheeks red, saying to come quickly and help their ma with the laundry, that she's feeling faint. Now, her ma faints often in the sun, so Lizzie sighed, stood up and asked me to stop by her house soon as I could to share the news. I hadn't told her it was from Fred, but she knew it was his handwriting on the envelope.

I opened the letter as Lizzie walked away. She looked back, and I raised my head, meaning to convey the tone of the letter was good. You could tell by the slope of his handwriting, the quality of the paper, torn from a paper bag, written in haste. I knew Fred was always one to sit quietly to write. He wrote a diary at home, sharpening his pencil carefully before he wrote and finding the perfect time to think. This recollection of him bending over his ideas as he put them on paper brought tears. I sniffed them back until I felt ready to read the letter.

Cousin Dawn,

Been a long time since I wrote. I have kept your letters under my pillow. It comforts me to know that you and my family are well. I think of you and hope the boys dance with you, for you are a shining star, my cousin. Have you given Matt a chance? I expect to hear from you about him. I demand to know your heart. You know you can't have me, for I am raring to run in foolish places. You aren't like that. You are my dearest cousin and closer to me than my sister or my sweet little Lizzie.

Families have to move on, mostly. We know each other too well to stay close, forever. If ever I kissed you, as I do Lizzie, my heart would smite me, and I could never look at you again. So it is best that we, being so fond of each other, are apart.

Let me tell you about my daily life. By now I have settled into a routine, except I spent the first weeks sleeping in a woodshed, until Mrs. G. decided I'd do for her full-time worker. She found me a room with Old Grumble; I call him that. He lives in a cabin by the sea in a cove, where you hear the waves on windy nights crashing. I have a small space—a bench to sleep on at night, but I am safe here, my Dawn.

I will tell you in all my letters of how awful it is to work for Mrs. G. I stopped her from beating her horses and showed her how speaking kindly to them each day makes them happier. These horses do everything for me. I don't have to lift a finger to them, only stare them in the eyes, speak sternly, and make sure they do my bidding. They draw wood for me now; I chop firewood, clear old limbs of trees from the woods. I spend the entire day working alone, then with Old Grumble at night. He smokes a pipe, I my cigarettes, and we play poker by the fire. I cook his dinner of fish and potatoes; we are a quiet pair. He does grumble about his bones hurting. I tell Mrs. G., when she comes into the barn after I have cleaned the stalls and fed the horses, that kindness to her animals is the least she can give—maybe that'll teach her something about humans. I don't care if she glares at me. She has flashing brown eyes and wild, curling, red hair. Grumbles says, "She dyes that hair; don't be fooled about her. She's old, in her forties, and wears pants, a hat, and carries a riding crop, even when she's not on a horse."

When I chided her about being cruel to her horses, I thought I lost my job. Only, she didn't fire me. She laughed and left the barn in a hurry. I watched her walk into her house and go around each room inside, by the looks of it. She turned on all the lights in her mansion, in every window that night.

She doesn't own just one place—she owns every house on the island, and nearly everyone works for her. She collects their rents the first of each month. If they cannot pay, she has no mercy for them. Everyone on the island helps each other, I am told, if one of them cannot have rent ready on time.

Dawn, I don't know how I can say this, but she's up to no good. Old Grumble grimaces when I mention her and says she is temperamental and not mindful how she hurts others and that she'll burn in hell, that's all. He gets to coughing when things upset him.

I will write you later. Don't say nothing yet to Lizzie, except tell her I miss her. She'd be horrified I had no sheets and only one change of clothes. That I eat the same food every day: fish.

Affect'ly,
Cousin Fred

I put this letter deep in my pocket, remembering to tell Lizzie certain things, not everything. That he had a dry place to sleep. That he thought of her. I wasn't going to say he missed her. Not yet. Lizzie might try to find him. I was sure Lizzie wanted to know if he was safe and if he had found a place to sleep. Love is, maybe, that you think of the simple things along with the complicated, like where your lover is sleeping, and then you can cover him with thoughts at night.

I thought of my pa before I slept, wishing he'd get over his sadness, hold me in his arms, let Mam know we were together again. You can't fill someone's heart if they close the lid, as she would say. I knew I had to wait for him to come home.

CB CB

I walked up the hill to Aunt's house. Uncle stood in the door. He asked me where I'd been, and I told him it was none of his right business, only I did what my chores demanded and then some. I showed him the basket of eggs from the store, and he gruffly cleared his throat. Some of his briskness is rude. I stepped past him, nearly treading on his feet. I put the items in the kitchen, went up to my room to get ready for morning chores. Dust of the road on my hands and hair.

I sat in the wicker chair by my window, looked across the valley. I calmed down from anger. I often hear him telling Aunt what to do in the house. I want to throw water on him when he starts bossing her. I reason that he has his days of worrying about his farm and making sure everything is in order. Why that makes him order her around, I don't understand. She weeps in her sewing room. When she comes out of this room, she takes a deep breath, as if she is resolved to love him better for all his weaknesses. That's not helping him, I sometimes think, after Uncle has come in to the kitchen from the barn, ranting about a dish being left on the kitchen table; shouldn't it be in the sink, he says, and what is his wife doing carrying the newspapers into the other room. He needs to read them, left where he put them this morning on the chair. Uncle has made Aunt timid, and that is sad to see.

People say Aunt was a shining flower when she was young. I looked through her photos in the album in the kitchen drawer. I wanted to whisper to her, "Don't let him make you feel terrible as if you did nothing right."

After some of his "nervous days," as Aunt called them, he and she'd go away for a few days, and he came back home calmed down. "Where do you go?" I asked her, when I first came to live with them. She shook her head, picked up her knitting, and watched me churn butter, her eyes staring hard at the wall. "His nerves get worse with age," she muttered. "But I love his true self, and that carries me through the bad days." I took on more of the chores for her, because she had sleepless nights worrying about him.

Mam told me Uncle wasn't raised a farmer. He came from a cultured family from further south, who went north to settle and raise a family. The depression left many people seeking cheaper land and places to live. I expect many folks came to Maine for these reasons and had anxiety over the tough climate and the toughness of work.

I loved Aunt almost as much Mam now, even though their personalities were different. Going to church, I knew, made Aunt happy. She said she felt loved in this small Church. Her god was within a building and a thunder god up above. She went home to her tyrannical husband, forgiving him for being an imperfect male. That was how, back then, I perceived religion.

These Nazis in our village, who had shattered our peace and trust for a while, seemed also imperfections of the universe. They represented a fearful, violent, male dominance. Spiders in Uncle's barn had webs ready for catching these imperfections. But Fred had the notion to bomb them out.

രു   ഇ

Mam said there are perfected beings called angels. They are life forms who have transformed themselves, like the saints, and live in the Invisible part of the universe. They can live permanently there, because they are pure. They help us on earth. The angels are rarely seen, she said. When Aunt had a bad day, crying in the sewing room, I talked to her about them. I told her, "They are able to be with us through the Principle of Light. When we think good thoughts, they are light-filled, and these angels can link with us and help."

"How do you know this, child? How do you remember so clearly what my sister said to you?"

"Very simple, Aunt Grace. Mam read many books to me. Such ideas are written in them. There is dark and light. When you die, you get to decide what direction to head for. She is where this light is, Aunt. You can be sure of that."

Mam said, ideas being universal, they are part of religions that took ideas and personified them. God is an idea personified. The Invisible is an idea; we cannot see it, as we cannot see God. Light is between the invisible and us. These light forms we call "angels" once were more material, as we, and someday we will be as light-endowed as they.

If Aunt cried too hard, I had to say something more concrete. "Auntie, I will take you outside in the fields tonight to show you the stars that Mam loved and show you which ones she said she would live on."

Aunt shook her head. Her younger sister was free spirited. Aunt remembered traveling with her, holding her from jumping into gondolas in Venice to surprise the gondola men. "Your mama was too beautiful for her own safety, let alone her wacky concepts of life."

"How do you stay at home now, Aunt Grace, and be content?"

"Because we traveled so much when young, I am perfectly glad to be here," she gently said. "You can't keep your whole life the way it was. It changes. I am full of memories I have of our father and mother, but that was their life which they shared with us for just a while. We left home to make our own way in the world. And time went swiftly, for they rest now in their graves, happy for their lives. I want to rest in mine with the same fulfillment."

I wanted to ask if everyone's life was to be peaceful. She read my thoughts, it seemed, for she gave me the sermon; here it is.

"Life brings you through turmoil to reconciliation. Sometimes you have to wait your whole life to achieve that with somebody." I saw a tear quit her cheek. "Sometimes you never succeed." I think she was thinking of her husband. I saw my uncle as being negative by trying to order and organize his environment because he was so upset inside. I asked, "Why is Uncle so upset?"

"Because he hasn't learned that the past is gone from him. It was his parents' life he loved, but it wasn't his own. He hasn't accepted how different is his. He is not a failure because he couldn't create a duplicate. His parents worked at a university, same as my parents. He has never forgiven himself for not taking their road, but that was a long time ago.

I visited Aunt in her sewing room while she worked on a sweater for him. Each stitch she knitted seemed to be a good thought toward this man, who was at this stage of life a bastard I hated.

"He's going through his turmoil, Aunt Grace," I said.

One thing about her and Mam, I could always say honest things to them. My own pa was the opposite of Uncle. Mama joked that he was a wimp, running after her, with no spine in his own back. I don't know which one is easier to live with, I thought, living with Pa away. Whatever their oddities, both these men seemed loved.

"When you get older, you'll understand," Aunt said.

ଔ   ଔ

I sat with the newspaper in my lap—war news. It was close at hand; becoming distant was the fear of Nazis returning to our village. I never thought any other news could eclipse our village fear.

The clock ticked, the woodstove hissed with pine slabs just cut, and the window was propped open by a screen. June bugs hit the screen and bounced off. Swallows flew close to the home, sweeping into the open hayloft door. A letter from Fred came in the mail.

Cousin Dawn,

I have more to write. I sit in the cabin, while outside the sea crashes, and a gas lamp illuminates this paper. The fire keeps me warm. Chilly wind blowing tonight. Old Grumble has a coon cat who watches mice very well, so she's allowed to stay inside the cabin. She is sitting by the fire with me.

I spent today cutting wood, loading it into Mrs. G.'s woodshed, and running errands to the grocery store. Then I helped Grumble with his wood. I stack the wood I cut for him beside his fireplace with the newspaper near the wood. We read the papers each night, keeping up on the news. No electricity, so can't listen to a radio with Grumble. We are far from the world out here. He isn't very literate, so I read to him. It is the usual evening routine. He only half understands what I say, I think. He is older than the villagers, and he knows far more than I think he does. It's like how the cat looks at me. I wonder if he knows something I don't know. He asks me each night: "Did you see anything unusual?"

I look at him strangely because he laughs and says I'll find out soon enough. Then he sighs and takes his pipe, smiles for a long time as he listens to me read. He blows the smoke into the air, watches it disappear and watches it appear again. Quite honestly, I am curious what he means.

News we read out here is the same as what you read. Only the newspaper gets mailed out here, so it is a few days late always. Grumble says to post my mail with Jimmy who works at the store and watch it put into the mailbag and make sure I watch until the bag of mail gets put on the boat. Make sure they tie it up before I trust my letters into anyone's hand. Those were many words coming from Grumble.

I asked him why he was telling me this. Aren't we safe out here on the island, far from the war? He just looked at me sideways and said: "Don't ever trust your letters in the hands of Mrs. G. Promise you won't tell her. I had to promise him, or he said he wouldn't talk to me anymore.

I promised him that, and he blows the smoke out more relaxed and nods his head. Maybe he is smarter than anyone thinks.

The wind hits the cabin as I write. The sea roars very hard. There are still peepers in the marsh nearby, and irises are blooming now in the swamp below the cabin.

Otherwise, it is very quiet out here, my cousin. Lizzie wouldn't feel safe here, I think, and might not think me safe.

Please tell her that I am all right. There are parts of life here that remind me of home. How the grocery store is where everyone meets. Ma Bean runs it and cooks soups and makes hot rolls for the lobstermen. They come in to buy tobacco and these rolls.

I wouldn't make a fisherman. It scares me out here at sea, Dawn. Nothing's more frightening than a storm and waves as tall as chimneys rising out here in the ocean.

Normally, on my time off, I walk over to the store, about a mile down the lane. Jimmy, when he sees me, waves. We sneak around the store building to the porch, where no one will see that I'm taking a longer lunch break than usual. It's where the professor sits at a table, and today guess who was with him! Old Grumble himself! And they were playing chess! I never dreamed the professor would be playing with the village idiot, as Grumble is called. The way the professor smiles and looks, kind of reserved and worldly, reminds me of both my grandfathers, Dawn. Remember, as uneducated as I am, they were refined and highly educated, but not even my pa could match his pa's lifestyle. I didn't see your ma or mine living up to their folks' way of life.

I smiled at the professor, and we talked about the island. He comes here for the summers, up from Philadelphia and says he's going to be living out here for good this year. Coming up here all these years for the summers gave him time to think and plan out his courses for his students the following year, but now he is retired, and his wife passed away. He thinks it's the best place to come back to.

These are the people so far in my life out here. Jimmy says he'll introduce me to his friends. And Marie keeps trying to get me to come to the Big House where she works. She is the maid, and there is a cook, only I haven't met her. Marie is dark-haired, very pretty, and speaks French because her family came from Quebec down to Maine.

Marie says she is frightened in the house with just her and the cook alone often. Mrs. G. goes on trips on her sailboat. We don't know where. I feel sorry for Marie but not sorry enough to spend nights sleeping in that house. The house is practically perched on the cliff. Can you imagine listening to the howling wind and sea crashing below the cliff, with the cove around the next corner? What about this cove? I asked her. I hadn't heard about it. "Nothing," she told me. It's hidden away from things.

The professor said there is a cave in the cliff near the cove, and pirates used to come into this as a secret harbor, when I asked him about it. He says Jimmy drives old cars off its cliff, too, for the tide to take out to sea. Cars do float in salt water, he says.

I am glad, Dawn, I can say so many things to you, not like a sister because that gets to Ma—if I were to write Sarah, she'd tell Ma everything—or to Lizzie, because she'd be unhappy for me and dreadfully annoyed about Marie and Mrs. G.

The other day, for instance, Mrs. G. was thrashing her horse again. It broke my heart. I grabbed the whip from her hand. Her eyes, the wild eyes she has, flashed, but she let me take the whip and reins.

She said for me to show her a better way to treat a horse. I took a deep breath, took a carrot from my pocket and let the poor beast smell it, calm down in great gasps. The horse finally let out a sigh which quivered her nostrils and shook her body. Then she ate the carrot. After that, it was easy to lead her out of the barn.

Mrs. G. asked me how I did that. I said it was easy. You have to love creatures and understand them. The horse didn't want to go outside. "It's windy," I told her. She'd prefer to be in her stall. Who wouldn't? I keep the stall very clean with fresh straw and hay for her.

Remember, cousin, how we rode the horses bareback before we hitched them up to the wagons for haying? We fed them and brushed them down, held them. We loved their breathing, the smell of them, and buried our noses in their faces. Remember? I told Mrs. G. that you, my cousin, breathe into a horse's nostril and then let it breathe into yours. Feel the prickly skin and stubs of hair and quiver of their breathing. The horse would do anything for you after that. Soul companions, I told her.

She laughed after that, said she needed a good laugh. We inlanders were quite strange. Did we also sleep in the horse's stall? I said that actually yes, when the horse was about to foal. We always did just that.

"You are a gentler man than I thought," she said. She thinks that since I chop wood all day, live with Old Grumble, that I am rough and crude.

What do you think, Dawn? I never considered myself rough and crude, or gentle, either. She is a bit daft, Jimmy says. I asked him what she does for a living, aside from taking in summer people in the Big House. He says she collects rents. That's how she lives during the rest of the year. She bought every place on this island, and with what means no one knows. She keeps rents cheap, but makes the islanders do their own repairs on the houses. Some say she's got stock that the depression didn't touch. Others say her husband died and left her a tidy amount to live on.

I don't care, Dawn, as long as she pays me, and I can have time away from my father's farm to get my thoughts together. Please give my love to my ma, pa and Sarah and my brother who is good-for-nothing. Just kidding. Kick his ass for me. He'll have the farm if he wakes up and starts to work on it. I don't want it. Does he have a girl yet, Dawn? Write me back.

Your cousin,
Fred

I put the letter under the bucket, stood by the barn window to look at the valley. I was upset that he was so concerned about Lizzie and not caring enough to be with her and rude about his brother and didn't ask me if Matt was still with me. I was interested who this Marie is in his life.

გ ღ

The church doors were open while the minister greeted the villagers. His sermon was simple. We sat quietly, Aunt watching the organist, and I drawing patterns on paper. Matt was in the next pew over with his Gran. I watched him, thinking I'd not tell him what I was doing after church.

I went alone to my own house. I left Aunt and wandered down the hill to cross the iron bridge. A recent rainstorm had made the river water rise. The thunder had shaken the valley last night. The water surged at breakneck speed under me. The bridge wobbled as I crossed it. I kept thinking my studio is where I'll be able to work. How it will be to claim that space now as mine—I remember I hardly could face this next step. I nearly choked with the thought of Mam. So alone I am, Mam.

The river raced towards me, and I hung over the bridge railings watching it. I let my tears fall in the racing water. When you hardly predict it, emotions hit, and the dear people you want back again, if just for a day, walk beside you. Mam was with me once more that early summer morning.

A dirt lane turned off the main road. Each rut seemed familiar, as if memory grew like the weeds in between the car tracks. Then I stopped. The field opened, full of buttercups, daisies, thick grass. The mountains shimmered.

There was my home, sitting off by a stand of fir trees, a stone wall surrounding it. Someone had scythed the front lawn. Pansies grew by the stone path. Ivy was cleared off the door, and windows sparkled. The sun shone on the front of the house, which faced southeast. The shutters had been painted a fresh green.

I walked to the door, expecting Mam to run out and throw her arms about me. I pictured her so vividly that I stepped back and gasped. Here was the fresh air, the granite front step, and no person there. I pulled the key from my pocket, turned the latch and entered. The old door creaked. I hadn't been inside for some years. I had to face this but almost couldn't.

Inside the front hall, the carpet and chair by the window still stood. Steep stairs went straight up. Every space was used; none was lost on stairs.

Time had hardly passed in this house, and I went to the door at the end of the hall, turned its handle and entered the kitchen. There was the slate sink and old pump in it, the kitchen table by the sink. The woodstove in a corner, the bookcase with my parents' books. Not a cobweb nor hint of dust. Beyond the kitchen was the porch with a grape arbor. Its vines were thicker than I remembered, its dark leaves hanging, tendrils reaching out for more space to grow.

I stood as if waiting for voices, a greeting for me to come back in time. The silence stifled me. I went to the sink and wept. For a while, that's all I could do. My cries racked my body; then came quietness, a worn-out mind. I had no one there to see my tears and not even a handkerchief. Wiping my nose on my dress sleeve, I went to sit beside the bookcase and read the titles.

I didn't question who might have cleaned my house. It was as I had left it when Pa said goodbye. We had closed the door behind us, looked back at the house, gone down the path, shut the front gate, walked past the stone wall.

Opening the cupboards, even the plates were still there, shined, and coffee cups polished. The silver in its drawer. The outhouse painted. I thumbed through a small history book, put it back, then decided to plan my studio space. It would have to be here, in her kitchen.

In the next room, the sofa and chairs remained in the same place as when we left them. The velvet sofa cushions, the ones that Mam and I had made, were fat and plumped up. There were other cushions on the floor, where Pa, Mam, and I sat by the fireplace. The desk under the stairs had its ceramic jar with pencils in it. There was paper in the drawers. I sat down to draw the plan for my space in the kitchen. I moved cautiously, feeling numb from the shock of reentering a beloved place with no one there. I even went looking for Pa, in case he had returned. No signs of his tobacco, no clothes, nothing there that smelled of him.

I didn't wish for him back yet. I didn't want distractions to my intent. I took paper and pencil and outlined my painting. I worked quietly, even reworking the lines. I wanted to dream into eternal time on my canvas. Time in which objects could emerge, but I could not yet abstract my ideas into the invisible and be there, where Mam now was. I let my tears hit the paper then rubbed them into the pencil print. Mix my tears with color, I thought. Saltwater and watercolor paints. They were not cheap, and I ruefully thought I'd chosen an expensive hobby, yet cast that thought away because eventually I'd sell my paintings. That was an inspiration— to let them go as children into the world.

Mam touched my arm, for a smile welled up from the heart; the day seemed full of possibilities. When you create, in due course you of course let go and hope for the best. Everything comes in due time. My worst fears were like nightmares. I had to place them at a distance and let morning give me its sun, and trust it to make visible the place of imagination where Mam had gone. Even if it were seen as I saw the furniture in front of me.

I watched the grape leaves. Wind took their points and turned them under to where their silver shone. "I am in the Universe mind, where ideas live, my Dawn. I'll give you ideas, as we shared them in the kitchen." I heard Mam say this.

As I held the paper with its sketch, I crossed the hall, opening the door to the parlor and adjacent sewing room. Here was furniture from the last century, from my grandmother's home. Gram's home had an attic still full with ornate items: mirrors, sofas, chairs, tables. My youngest aunt had the house now. She was married to a lawyer. She viewed me as trouble, born wild with Mam's free spirit. I preferred to live near my old home rather than in the town with its houses backed into each other. I always need meadows to glance over and let my mind drift to the ridge of mountains.

I peeked into Mam's sewing room, as if to find a new project under way. I was spooked, believing she'd slipped into the house to work quietly, but the room was bare, the fabric long cleared away and needles and pins off the table. Yet, the sewing machine remained. I touched its treadle with my foot, and it made a clack as the wheel turned. I would give this away, I thought—it is an encumbrance now to me, for I do not sew enough to justify its place here. I thought Aunt's church the place for it. I'd keep my paints and supplies in this room, my plans and ideas on paper, and paint where it was bright and warm, where I could remember conversations. The laundry room, off the sewing room, connecting to the kitchen, still had the old front-load washing machine, the deep sink to soak Pa's trousers before Mam washed them. I would save this; maybe I'd live here permanently.

I looked up the steep stairs but did not ascend them. It was too much for today, to see the two bedrooms, the guest room at the top of the stairs—it had been called "the fainting room," where ladies from the past century could go up and loosen their corsets and breathe for a while.

I pictured my clothes in the drawers; I knew some of them were still there. Sudden grief is like this. You leave in a hurry, with a forced decision, because sadness does this. You leave things behind, or you tidy up, making sure a caretaker looks after your place, if you have it paid for, as Pa had; you walk down the path, shut the gate until you can deal with it all. I have come back, able to see into the very beginning of my future.

Another time, I thought, furtively casting a glance at the steps going up. I held my hand to the rail and didn't let my feet get ahead of me, afraid lest I be tempted to go against my wishes. I grasped my paper and pencil, went out the front door and sat on the granite step to look at the stone wall. Larkspur, roses and foxgloves grew there. Someone had even weeded the flower bed. I didn't think of anyone living who could have done it. That was far from my mind. I was a slip of a child running outside, full of beauty of a perfect day with Mama, Pa, the horses in the near field. How would I have known the world had to transform me, battling the elements of heartache.

Aunt took me once to her minister, who tried to counsel me, telling me it was my determination and vision of good things to come to me that would take me onward. The Lord, he said, will hold you in the palm of His hands.

This morning I held my home. I breathed in deeply and saw the dewdrops lingering in the shadows under the fir trees, glades of the sun as it rounded the corner of the house into midday.

Walking back to Aunt, I began my plan of earning money for paints, paper, brushes, and setting aside enough each week from my allowance and in a month's time ordering the first supplies. It would work. The past seemed to lift with the river mist, off into white clouds.

Matt saw me sitting on the steps of the store. No one was about because it was Sunday. I was resting before climbing the hill to the farm. He waved, hurried over.

"Where've you been? How's my girl?"

"Out for a walk, Matt. Nothing much doing." I didn't feel like talking, even with him.

"May I walk up the hill with you?"

"I won't object." Since he was busy on his farm with the planting, I'd not seen much of him. Being apart, working hard, cleared my thoughts. I didn't want to rush into such closeness. There were girls desperate to get married before their men might be off to war. No one will go to war from our village, I fiercely thought. The war was making us idiots. Men smoking on porches, talking about staying or leaving. Men are ridiculous creatures, I thought. Imagine discussing whether to stay or leave, like there were parts of drifting air. Would women in a beauty parlor, talking away, ask, shall we stay or leave? I have not mentioned our village beauty parlor, where Mrs. B. and her friends go once a week to have their hair shampooed or permed. It was next door to the library, in a woman called Dee's home.

I thought of Fred, who seemed unconcerned about the war. He was truly, I thought, running from Lizzie. I coughed, which made Matt, walking beside me, jump. Lizzie wanted to go straight from her family to raising one of her own.

Fred and I were alike, running—from or to—our own things. I had my own space and ideas of life. Yet, contrary to him, I was not fleeing from the mainland to an island. I ran alongside a relationship, Matt beside me. Ran right into my home.

03   80

As we trudged uphill swallows dipped over the fields. A pickup truck struggled with its gears up this road. It was the farmhand delivering groceries for Mrs. B. He raised his hand, waved a cigarette.

"That old Plymouth," Matt remarked. "Ten years and taking the hills."

Roads went up every incline on this side of the river. The mountain view stretched into an infinite northern land. The other side of the river was flat, where my home sat, warmer for gardens.

Matt asked, "Heard from Fred?"

I lifted my head. Not only were swallows after insects, but the cows jumped, sauntered across landscapes of mole ridges, grass hillocks. A horse grazed, ears perked up to run from these cows.

I had the most recent letter stuffed in my pocket; I wasn't sharing it with anyone. I didn't know what to do about my worries for Fred. I pretended my sweating hand holding the guarded letter would never release its grasp.

He'd seen my hand go into the pocket. "Want to share it?"

I didn't answer. I measured our steps, how offbeat they were. His front right foot strutted out before my left foot left the ground behind me. I felt out of alignment. We walked in silence. Matt had sense, I thought, to wait for my answer. A dark cloud shaded the sun. Wind came over the hilltop; a fox jumped across a stone wall. Squirrels chattered; oak bark had grooves worn from winter. Moisture ran from these seams.

I said simply that maybe he could read it. I didn't mean yes. Maybe was only a possibility. My hand was not going to let go of that paper easily. My uncertainty brews confusion at any time in my life. I had unintentionally made Matt take the lead. I remember wisdom of these hills in this sunshine saying simply, let it be.

He pulled me to the edge of the road, under the chestnut tree. Bees took the last pollen from the fading flowers. Its large leaves extended on branches across the road. "Come on, you've been holding it all inside of you and taking Fred's actions as your responsibility, even. You're protecting Lizzie, your aunt and uncle, not letting anyone know the details. You assure us he's safe. Safe from what?"

"Safe from keeping on running, Matt."

The mountains clouds left dark patches in the curves of highland meadows. The valley looked up. Wind floated across the hillside. It was the place we knew so well. Matt shook his head. "He can't obviously keep on running. No one is chasing him. If anyone, they'd be after your uncle." He shut his mouth. I opened mine in wide astonishment. I didn't want to know what he was going to say. Could it be Uncle had masterminded the dynamiting? I'd always thought it was Fred, and now Fred was taking the blame to save Uncle, whose silence and anxiety had increased. It had only made life harder for Aunt.

"Let's say Fred is safe and leave it at that," Matt said.

I fumbled words. There was nothing secret for long. It'd turn out the entire village had backed up Uncle in this idea, the best way, they agreed, to get the Nazi hornets out. Bomb them. Anarchists, it was said of us.

The newspapers had stopped running the story. The government didn't come after the village for acting on its own. No one was arrested. The landlord of the house took full responsibility for destroying his own home, no insurance asked for. It was dropped. The name "Nazi" blew away, as if it had never been. The German newspapers and letters, which the housekeeper had stolen from them as evidence if anything came to court, weren't inquired into. The government, the village men said, as they smoked their cigarettes on the store porch, wanted nothing to do with it.

"Here, Matt. Maybe it's good to show it to you, so that you keep quiet with me."

He raised his eyebrows and took the letter. While he read, I closed my eyes, thinking where Pa must be and, if he could be here, what would he be saying about the politics of our everyday lives. Revolution, he'd say. Destruction has no purpose except in its moment. Contribution has to wait until the right timing. We don't know what this is leading to.

Matt still held my hand, gripping my fingers tightly now as he read Fred's letter. I sighed; maybe it'd help me sleep better at night, sharing Fred's life.

He finally put it down, picked it up once more to read a part, then stopped halfway through to read it again.

We were in emptiness, watching buzzards flying looking for dead carcasses. I was focusing on my plan to paint and how to earn needed income. I'd about worked it out by the time Matt found me by the store. I was growing annoyed now that Fred was interfering with my thoughts. Fred, who had run from both Lizzie and me. He was more interested in me, and that was the frightening thing, we being cousins.

Matt said, "If I could leave my mother's farm, I'd go out there and bring him back. Something doesn't sound right out there." I waited for him to continue.

"You know this feeling when you step outdoors at night, and you sense a bear is out there or a fox. The hairs rise on your arms. You step into a home you've not been in for years, and it's clean, tidy, waiting for you, and you wonder who did that, since no one lives there."

I grabbed the letter, stuffed it back into my pocket. From his eyes, I was frightened he desired to kiss me, take me in the meadow grass. "We are only friends," I told him. "I don't wish to speak anymore about my cousin."

Life was about survival, not yielding to someone else. I was not inquisitive of what life was beyond the basic routines of each day. At dances the girls who were my childhood friends gossiped about relationships. I laughed at this futile sense of maturing. Was Matt courting me and did I realize this? They said this was a fact. I said no; let me alone. They nearly spat on me then. At least half the girls were after this friend of mine. It was as if they said to me: Are you above us that you don't care for a good-looking man who favors you?

I shunned the dances if I could. Aunt tried to get me to go by making gorgeous dresses for me. She said I'd blossom into a rose soon, and when that happened I'd understand those girls. She took me to the doctor to make sure my health was fine. She didn't want to miss out on anything she could be doing to help me along in life as her sister's only child, the sister now in heaven. She whispered something to the doctor, and he shook his head.

"She's fine." He said this to her face. "After a deep loss or trauma, a person can distance things; we call it 'disassociation.' They are looking at people, events, from further away—that one would normally feel close to in life."

He looked at me. "Dawn will be fine. She'll make something of herself, you'll see. She sees beyond what is viewed. She sees things as if she is looking down on them and gets on fine. She will have a harder time making a mother of herself, a farm lady, mind that well. Don't push her to be what she isn't fit for."

Aunt looked away as he said this. He had known her for some years. Maybe she had forced herself to be what she wasn't cut out for.

He continued, "Life comes, molds us; we carve it. Dawn had severe trauma, and you her aunt have been the kindest person in the world to give her a home and a family and your love."

When he said that, showing me how he remembered me since birth and understood my earliest part of life, I wept. Aunt held me until I felt I melted into her own heart. When we walked up the hill, I was more into my life in some small way, as if it were only a matter of undoing my knots.

That afternoon Matt and I went to my home. I saw how he blushed, turning away as I walked inside. My hair covered my face that day. I saw through one eye.

"You did all that for me?" I asked.

"Yep," he sounded awkward, fumbling for the right words. "My ma and I want you to feel you have your home back."

I sat on the floor with a pillow. I couldn't stop talking. Everything I was planning came in paragraphs of ideas of paints, canvas, how I'd make money enough to do this, and I'd paint on Sundays, my time alone. Wasn't he encouraging me to paint?

"Stop," Matt said.

We walked around the house. Taking me in his arms beside the garden gate, he held me as you hold a day lily, which blooms for one day. When do you pick it? Early morning.

ଔ   ଔ

That night, after I added figures in my notebook on how to afford art items, I pulled Fred's letter from my dress pocket. Reading it, I pictured our village dances with girls in handmade dresses; Aunt had made mine, which to please her I wore to her church. It was short-sleeved and reached below my knees; a shawl added warmth. I felt well dressed, thus I didn't understand why people turned to look at me when I entered church. I asked the minister to forgive my appearance, since many people stared. He broke into a smile and said it was because I looked like an angel.

Aunt had put her arms around me when he said that. When we were out of earshot, she told me my hair needed to be braided next Sunday; I will be less conspicuous. She added she'd hate to cut my hair. I gave her a hug, said goodbye, walked alone to her house.

Inside I had hung my shawl behind the kitchen door. I talked aloud: "Fred, what are you doing upsetting us?" I spoke to the wallpaper. The flower pattern stared back at me.

Matt hadn't read the whole letter. He'd become distracted. Perhaps he wished to find Fred, I reflected. He'd added quickly something he hadn't intended to tell me, in his roundabout way, that helped make my home mine again. I curled up in bed on the sheepskin to re-read the letter; I heard the sea breaking. The water was clear, reflecting the clouds and mountains here inland.

I kept all his letters safe from anyone. Meanwhile another one came.

Dear Dawn,

Old Grumble sleeps by the fire, and I have time to write you before sleeping on my bench.

If I write you every few days, I do so not knowing if all my letters will get to you. The sea is choppy, the mail boat comes once weekly, lobster boats aren't doing the long sea run except on special occasions. The small ferry goes once monthly.

Mrs. G.'s maid, Marie, is friendly to me and brought me inside the Big House when Mrs. G. wasn't there. I don't know who she sees off the island. Marie asked if I wanted to see a room, which was locked except when Mrs. G.'s special friend visited. When I asked who the special friend was, she was unable to tell me. "He wears a uniform and speaks German."

When she said that, I jumped to the ceiling of that hall. I gulped, looked around me, then followed her down a dark passage lit only by her candle. She unlocked a door from a collection of keys on a chain.

In this room was gold. There were paintings with gold-leafed frames. I am no artist, Dawn, but you would have loved these paintings. Remember the story your mam told of King Midas and the curse of the golden touch? I believe Mrs. G. has that touch. I backed out from this room in horror. Marie pushed me back in, saying I was silly, get my feet under me, that she'd explain what I was seeing. There were gold watches on a table, gold coins scattered as if someone dropped them there. Gold leaf decorated the borders of walls under the ceilings. Gilt porcelain bowls rested on another table. Other small items far too numerous to mention.

Marie made me promise not to tell Mrs. G. I'd seen this room or relate this to anyone on the island, not even the professor. Certainly not Old Grumble.

"Where did this come from?" I asked. I'd heard stories of pirates hiding loot on Maine islands. I thought I'd found a den. Marie said that there is a cave on the island where more is hidden, waiting to be brought up here. A cave in the cliff; I knew of this from the professor.

"Have pirates brought this here?" I asked.

Marie said no. "At eleven o'clock tonight, meet me on the cliff by the cove," she said." It is important to see what happens next."

I can hear you gasping, Dawn. It is important you get this, if some evil befalls me. I like Marie very much, but you know I think of you and Lizzie the most, and please don't mention Marie to her.

In order to meet her at 11 p.m., I had to pretend to go to sleep and wait until Grumble slept. Then I tiptoed out of his cabin, skirted the forest along the island road until it came to the cove. I climbed the cliff. The moon was bright. I heard Marie whispering, "Come here."

I crawled to hide beneath the sea peas and vetch. This is a good enough shelter, although slightly damp. We breathed very quietly. On clear nights with the full moon, sound travels like the smallest rustle of waves at a distance on the shore.

The cove water glistened as a porpoise surfaced. I focused on it, because I had never seen such a creature. The more I looked, the larger it became. It turned into a large hulk of silver, which rose as if by magic from the sea. It drifted further into the cove, and a hole in the top of it rose up. A man climbed out, and someone rowed a boat to him and brought him ashore. We were higher up than they were but close enough to hear talking. The moon showed the man, who was dressed in an officer's uniform, and they spoke German together. They saluted each other saying what we'd heard on the radio in Mr. B.'s store: *Heil Hitler!*

Dawn, I am afraid. I ran from them in our village, and they are here. What shall I do? I will catch the ferry home if I can, soon.

Marie was trembling, saying that they will kill us if they suspect we saw them. I believe her.

We watched them reach the house, enter it, and saw a light shine in the two upstairs windows. Marie said Mrs. G. had returned a few hours before the officer's arrival. Mrs. G. has a sailboat, I remember now, and Marie says she takes it out some days. She usually sails alone. The seas off here are often wild with white-tipped waves.

Marie told me the officer stores the gold in the house and a nearby cave. Mrs. G. wears one of the gold wristwatches. It is such a lovely watch, Marie says, the officer gave it to her. Yet, think how it must have once belonged to another woman. She strokes the watch constantly when she wears it. Is she thinking about the officer? Marie wonders. What do you think, Dawn?

Marie is older than I and is from a village on the coast. She isn't from inland as we are. Her papa will come for her at a moment's notice, although it will take a day to get out here. I asked her how he will know. Marie said she keeps a carrier pigeon.

Please hide this letter, cousin. I'm in over my ears here now. I keep chopping wood for the old lady. She isn't that old, either. If she doesn't fancy the officer, she sure does me. I will either come home to you or mind myself out here.

Love,
Cousin Fred

I turned out my light. Opened the curtains to see the stars; Mam lit up the sky, so I could view this firmament. "How are you, Mam? Are you looking back on your earth memory, to when I was a baby, just born, and you held me?"

Mam replied, "Ah, even further back, Dawn. I am in memory of before you came to us, of when your pa and I were in college." Her voice faded. There was a glow in her memory of Pa. I could see her smiling. I fell asleep with the stars in my face, her voice in my ear, and Fred's letter under my pillow.

☞   ☜

Summer brought a return to daily life in our village. The excitement over the Nazis died down. They didn't return to live here. No other strangers moved into any homes. I guess they would be scrutinized very hard. Occasionally the sheriff stopped by Mr. B., where they both stood on the porch, smoked cigars.

Meanwhile, my plans were underway about raising money. I grew herbs and flowers at my house and sold them Saturdays in front of Mr. B.'s. They were liked, and I did well that summer.

By the end of August, I had bought oil paints, turpentine, canvas, frames, watercolors, and an easel. I had wood to heat the stove in late fall and winter. Finally I could work in my studio, designing a painting. It took hours to dream its form.

It took time to build up a market. In retrospect, persistence paid off. I started in small ways, with the idea to show my paintings in galleries. My paintings, although I had to market them to pay for art materials, were for my own healing; they helped me eventually let go of my mother. I saw her distantly, as if connected by a fine string. I could pull her down with it, release her up again.

In my paintings a detail, say a flower, had a landscape in back of it, a hillside view. A butterfly and the valley with spring bringing it color after a harsh winter. The detail created images of infinite expansion.

I read all my parents' books, for even Pa collected amounts of reading, stored in the attic for winter evenings. I put my book down, pulling out another of Fred's letters. By now I had several shoeboxes of them under my bed. He wrote his parents separately sometimes, only his father, outlining tasks for Jeremy to do on the farm. He asked after each cow and described what needed to be done for their health. As much as he cared for the farm, he told his father now that he never wished to be a farmer. Jeremy would need the farm. He, Fred, would help Jeremy whenever needed.

Aunt told me that Uncle put the farm in both his sons' names. He stated that the village needed farmers staying home from war. He believed food would be needed, and the government couldn't make those who farmed the land leave their holdings. He maintained that food had to stay locally grown, and remain wholesome for people. He wasn't making an antiwar statement, only one of necessity. If young men left who took care of their family's farm, then our society would crumble.

"If that's gone, the whole foundation of food—if our stores start selling everything from other states and countries, even a thousand miles away, which is starting to happen, then our village is gone, except for those with cars to take them to jobs elsewhere." Uncle stood on the store porch, calmly smoking a pipe, with a handful of men sitting on chairs, listening to his lecture.

"No, we have to be strong here and keep prices down and keep our food coming into the stores. This war storm abroad is capturing everybody's mind and making young men run to it, as if it's the answer to their own day-to-day discontents." Several older men assented and blew smoke out in a dragon's puff.

I was there at his talks only to listen. I knew both sides of my uncle and didn't like the way he behaved at home with Aunt, but realized he was admired out of the home. He probably would run to war to get away from the domesticity of home, if he didn't have a farm. I shook my head with that thought and wandered away from the talk.

I needed to focus on my life. I wasn't going to marry Matt, at least not yet. Not when I had no desire to share my home with anyone and none to live in his. He hadn't asked me. We weren't at that part yet.

I watched the swallows diving into the fields, catching insects. They ranged high in their motions. Wind blew them, but they picked those bugs at swift speeds.

It seemed Matt and I had, without discussing it, decided not to fear for Fred. I don't remember how we came to that point of letting him be. Our conversations began to leave him out. He only interrupted our thoughts. We had no avenue to go on with our own happiness. Matt was with me on Sunday afternoons. I liked someone to talk to me as I painted. "You'll sell soon, he said, you'll sell your first painting and make enough to buy the next canvas." He was right, for I did, but that comes later.

The kitchen-studio kettle whistled. I ran my fingers through my hair. "Rats hide in it," Matt had laughed, as he took my hair by the handful to sniff it. "Stinks of oil and turpentine," he had grinned.

My hair now came to my calves. I didn't know what to do with it but leave it grow. I wore baggy pants, an old sweater covered in paint smears. Other things, like underwear and socks, I daily washed and hung them on the porch. As little chores to do as possible—this was my painting world.

After the kettle whistled, I made tea and went off by myself to read Fred's new letter.

Dear Dawn,

The German officer went up to the house. His "boy," the young man in the rowboat, accompanied him, as I told you in the last letter. A cold wind blew as I sat on the cliff, watching with Marie. I put my arms around her. Now don't tell Lizzie this— to keep us warm, and we waited until we felt it was safe to get up and leave. I went back to Old Grumble's cabin, and Marie sneaked into the back door of the Big House; she told me she'd done it many times and not to worry. Mrs. G. knew she went out late to listen to music with people and dance. This isn't the same country dancing out here. Marie brings the records with her from the coast, of swing music.

I waited until she waved at me from a room upstairs in the Big House. She wanted me to know she was safe, but if I wanted to I could come in the back door up to her bedroom. I never been to it and never will. I didn't go, so don't anyone get the wrong ideas.

Grumble was asleep when I snuck in, and I went quietly to my bench, pulled the blanket over me and slept by the smoldering fire.

Next morning Marie tapped on the window, excited, I could tell. She held up a gold bracelet for me to see. I stepped out, whispering to her so Grumble wouldn't wake, and asked where she got it.

She said the German officer gave it to her at breakfast this morning to thank her for putting flowers in his bedroom. Mrs. G. had told him the maid did the floral arrangements.

She knew it was early and Grumble slept late, so could she talk for a moment. She was very nervous. "What will I do with it?" I told her she'd best keep it safely underneath her mattress.

The officer was there for two days. Each night he and the boy rowed out to the U-boat and came back to sleep in the Big House. Marie and the cook treated them well, as guests always were in the mansion, no matter their nationality.

When they left, Marie told me to follow her to the locked room. This room, which she opened always with her bunch of keys, had new plates of china, gold-leafed on the edges, and new paintings with gold frames. Then there were piles of knickknacks arranged on tables, spilling over onto the floor. Gold coins, more wristwatches, as if they were taken off of people and stashed in other people's pockets and not wanted anymore. Left to be in piles of memories here. I stared at them for quite a while until Marie nudged me to look at something different.

If I say this to you in just these few words, quickly written to you, Dawn, it is because I know your imagination can create the picture. I am confused as to what to do and how to stay out of it. There is peace in not knowing too much more than what you see.

Marie had to get me out of the house quickly, because she heard Mrs. G. coming in from the stables. I dodged out the back door by the kitchen. The cook looked at me from the corner of her eye, and I expect she knew about this room, too, and kept quiet. I almost thought she winked at me.

Marie told me the officer speaks about the wonderful world that Hitler imagines he can make, an efficient world power, with satellite countries under German world power, as England has in its empire. He said we won't know much difference in our everyday life in this country when Germany takes over America. In fact, he said, our economy will be much better. Germans knew how to do things well. Any opposition to Hitler in this country, even in tiny villages in Maine, and he stared hard at Marie, will be crushed.

Marie said she interrupted him, even though Mrs. G. kicked her under the table, and asked him how Germans would crush our tiny villages. He replied that it would be simple. "See those cliffs, my dear? See that sea?" The sea to dump us, the woods to light the homes on fire.

Marie said she shivered. Mrs. G. only laughed at him and said we will wait and see whether he, a brilliant, handsome man, was capable of this. Of course she was joking, but he took it seriously and smiled at her.

Now the biggest news is this. I hide it in the small print, because I don't want it to glare out if someone glances at this letter. This is the news: Mrs. G. is giving him fuel for the U-boat.

I asked her, "How? How with everyone watching?" There is a large tank on the hill behind the village. It has fuel in it for the lobster- and ferry-boats. The fuel boat fills it up once a month. A long hose goes from the tank to the harbor, a short distance. At night, when the village sleeps, the long hose extends into the harbor for the U-boat, which goes from the cove into the other cove. No one has ever seen it there, according to Marie. I hesitate to write this, because I know Grumble knows about this. Sometimes, when I think he is sleeping, he is out and about, walking the dirt roads of the island.

Do the islanders know about the Nazis? I mention Old Grumble, although I believe many of them have a hunch that something is going on, but I doubt they link it to a distant country's citizen coming to this island. All the islanders pay rent to Mrs. G. and don't want to give up their homes, so they comply, and after all it is an island far out at sea, so what does it matter? If a Nazi comes here often, stays with Mrs. G., fuels up and gets out, it is not infringing on their lives. Her lover, is what I think they'd say. So what?

We are in control of our destiny, Dawn. I keep chopping wood, mending wharves, keeping to my own business, and I won't be touching this Nazi. I believe they are infiltrating everywhere, our village, and now out here.

I have an idea that Mrs. G. could be a spy, watching him for our government, and he not knowing it. She could be playing two games, giving him fuel, information, if she has any, and that is a laugh, for out here there's nothing, and then she'd be telling our government what he tells her.

Do not worry about me. Old Grumble has a safe cabin, and we have a gun here.

I am tired and ready to sleep. Matt writes me that you are

setting up a place in your own home to paint. I am proud of you, cousin. Matt is a kind person, too gentle to be joining the armed forces, which he is doing soon, but don't tell him I told you. He thinks you need time to grow without his feelings about you. He loves you, but he is at either needing to settle down or do something else. Remember, he is older than you and will wait for you. That is the problem with this war. It is too big an excuse to not face reality at home. The thought of fighting is an emotion, and that has its own reality. He may get killed. I told him not to go. You know your own mind enough, and he doesn't have to run away from you. Once this war is over, our generation, Dawn, will settle down, those of us who stay alive.

Sleep on that. Marie says she is afraid for our lives on this island with this Nazi. Remember, Grumble and I are armed.

Aff'tly,
Cousin Fred

As I read this, I made chicory coffee in two old mugs. I decided it was okay to let Matt see this one. I'd take my cup outside when he came to the last bit, about himself; he'd be alone to read it. He wouldn't have to look into my eyes.

I thought on the difference in our ages. How right now, at this time, I could only be the way I was. I couldn't become a different person or process what I couldn't feel. I needed time to understand what Fred meant by "reality at home." He knew I wasn't wanting to settle and raise a family just yet. Yet, how strange it wasn't quite that way, looking back. Nothing seems clear until you see it gone by and are years from it. Then perhaps you look at your own maze with clarity and see why you took a certain point of view, only to have life defy you.

Well, Matt came in, and I let him read Fred's letter. He touched my shoulder, which drew me closer to him. He dropped into an old chair. I sat in his lap, comfortable, secure, wishing no change to the tenuous control I had of my own life. He ran his rough hand across my arm. A hesitant movement, bringing his hand higher than my elbow.

"So, you are thinking of leaving?" I asked.

He looked from the window to the field of flowers in front of my house. "When you're ready, started your paintings, and . . ."

He lost his thought. He meant to say if Pa came home. I instinctively knew this thought hung in the air here. If he returned, would it be my home? Would I want then to live with Matt? We had never talked about this. If Pa came home, of course, I'd keep house for him, get him back on his feet, back into his vet job. I had many nights of thinking about my pa. Yet Matt caught my hair as he always did, in his hand, and said, "I am meaning you, I love you, my darling."

I melted then for just a moment. It was as watching the butter disappear in my Aunt's frying pan. I had to quickly put the eggs in. My soul here had to have another ingredient mixed into this. It was too easy to disappear. I turned my head from his lips. I wasn't able to reach them.

Love is not a physical place. Walls around me held a material grief, not the transient presence of young passion. Or so I perceived it like that then. Perhaps time is part of love, which melts it into malleable clay. Something I couldn't let go.

Matt turned away; robins held onto vines outside the window.

"Maybe, someday, you'll love me," he said.

☙ ❧

Fred wrote again. I tried to keep from discussing him with Matt, but more letters from him meant redoubled thoughts of him. My affection was expressed in this line: Mam—in heaven—Pa, then Fred. He remained the only tangible part of my heart and soul to whom I could open. Alas no, I say that too easily. He was not there anymore; he came between Matt and me now. He, dealing with his Nazi on that dark island. What care I? Did that terror emerge in a night dream as mystery, possibility that unknown annihilation could come from this evil? I termed it evil.

This kind of despair goes beyond anything I can describe. He who is kin within the network of family. This love stretches far beyond the short time that Matt had loved me. It goes back to our ancestors, whose portraits hung on Aunt's walls. Centuries of farm folk, tied to land, work, caretakers of a community.

Dear Dawn,

Following our discovery of more gold in the room, Marie is careful not to take me there again. Catching us, Mrs. G. would have us thrown over the cliff.

Through the windows we watch Mrs. G. dance with the Nazi at night. She puts on a record, on the self-winding gramophone; her red hair sticks out wildly, and her red lipstick and red nails look like a lobster claw ready to pinch him. One evening we saw them dance, and he held her with his lips stuck onto her face. It was like a whelk clinging to a rock.

Marie sucked in her breath and held my hand. My heart jumped like the fish, more than I care to admit. Her parents count on her keeping this job, sending money back to help with the food bill in Rockport each month. She has younger siblings and an older brother.

Marie worries that I am getting very skinny. She wants to ask Mrs. G. to give me a room in the Big House over winter. Mrs. G. nearly loses her mind over Marie—Mrs. G. is so all over the place. She cannot keep track of this maid. She knows the Nazi officer likes her maid, so she doesn't dare treat her cruelly. I forgot if I told you the Nazi gave Marie a gold bracelet, which Mrs. G. is extremely upset about, which makes Marie laugh. She secretly says to me she will sell the bracelet on the mainland to help her family.

Sometimes I lie on my bench at night thinking of Lizzie and Marie, as if they were sisters. If I were ready to settle down, I'd have to toss a coin heads or tails to decide on which of those two I'd have. I couldn't rationally make the decision.

Dawn, sweet and quiet cousin, I'm glad you can read through these words I can't say to anyone else, and thank you. I am glad you are starting a life for yourself and considering what will make you happy. You and I are similar, only I can't find out what will make me happy. That is the most important thing in life. If you are happy, Dawn, the world smiles too. I could be forever happy with you.

We are alike in that we are thinking of ourselves, the passion of being true to what one needs to do to be happy. Only you know what it is. You have found the ingredient for your well being. I am only running away still. Running to what? To this island, a place of a Nazi's temporary happiness. The secure place for his gold. And he delights in the relationship on this island with my vivacious employer.

I walk along the cliff at night. The U-boat has been here a week. I watch things taken back and forth from the house to the U-boat at night. There are now two other men who have come to stay at the house.

Mrs. G.'s cook is not my sort. She has short dark hair and

speaks only French with Marie, and if she speaks English she is not intelligible. Mrs. G. demands they speak more slowly.

Marie brings me these stories at night. At dinner, the Nazi scolds the cook and says in his country the French are seen as fickle people. First they like the Russians, he says, then they like the Americans, then, he says—they really only desire their wine and lovely women. Yvette, the cook, blushed, put her hands on her hips, swished her starched white apron as if scaring chickens away and told him to change his opinion, because her French family from Canada has lived in Maine for over a century and has nothing to do with the France that he is talking about.

The cook said, "France is our homeland, but the New World is our home. You hate us because we escaped from poverty and oppression in France? *Oui?*" She made a "poof" sound with her lips puckering, Marie said.

The cook said she wouldn't mind poisoning Monsieur Germany sitting here being served by her in Maine.

Marie nearly exploded but turned to the wall of photographs.

The German officer had placed his photo there, she saw suddenly. It was a framed picture with a symbol exactly like the one on his insignia. Marie said it reminded her of the symbols of the Freemasons, which her father belongs to. Marie sometimes sneaks into their meeting room and sees the symbols hanging on the wall. She'd be killed if they knew she'd done this, she told me in a solemn tone. Of course I knew that was probably an exaggeration. What I am telling you about us being killed for what we know is truth.

I told her not to speak like that because all the men in my village belonged to that organization, and along with the Grange movement it gave them a lot of support in their businesses and farms. Marie said that I have been properly brainwashed, that thank goodness she is not blind to this.

When she wrote her father about the sign the German wears, he wrote her back to be careful. "It is a distorted sign, and because of that it is dangerous to look at. Do not stare at it," he said. "Turn from it immediately; promise me," he asked her. He explained the symbol was taken from ancient rituals. They have no idea how wrong it was to take it out of its context.

Nevertheless, Marie did look at that symbol, trying to decide what to do with it. Leaving it there on the wall, she brought stones from the seashore and placed them underneath the picture on the chest of drawers. She said it made her feel better about the spider—that symbol resembles a spider, she explained to me. Best to leave it hang on the wall.

The German officer pushed out his belly as he laughed. Maria said she nearly forgot the symbol in watching his reaction. He was saying that it's strange to place stones underneath his symbol. He lifted his head as he arrogantly spoke, which made Marie angry. Marie told him that something as foreign as that symbol hanging on a wall in Maine needs some beauty surrounding it. At that point, Yvette said she'd add to the contribution from Maine and took sand out of her apron pocket. Mrs. G. asked her where she got that sand.

"From the beach, Madame."

"Yvette and I lie on the beach on our breaks and put shells in our pockets." Marie hastily added.

I told her that reply would make Mrs. G. suspicious that she might know about the U-boat.

Marie's reply made the German officer nervous. Mrs. G. was in a cross temper. She wasn't the center of attention. She had Marie tidy the table, take dishes to the kitchen, and banished Yvette to the kitchen to wait to bring out the dessert. Marie no longer shares meals with Mrs. G. and her German guest. A formality has been established whereby the maid and cook now eat in the kitchen.

Mrs. G. and the officer ate, drinking wine to finish the meal and rubbing their fingers along the wineglass rims. Marie notices that when they have nothing to say, they make sounds from the glasses. Then laugh together. Marie can peer through the crack of the swinging door between the dining room and kitchen. When they spoke, it was quietly so no one heard except for Marie, of course.

France was a comical land, the Nazi was saying. It has no strong government and weak military, and although a robust economy, has been swayed to sign a pact with Russia and Czechoslovakia, signifying Russia's fear of Germany. "We triumph," he said. "We have no fear."

Mrs. G. broke a cracker to wipe up spilled wine on the table. She said that peace was never what Hitler wanted, was it? She stroked the Nazi officer's chin, and Marie kept peering through the crack.

The Nazi officer said, "Of course not. Hitler wants to reshape continents, not bother about border politics of European countries. If you think he wanted peace, that is a big miscalculation. Political power is one aim, advancing the evolution of mankind another. Destroying subhumans is the next move. Here is a book for you to read about that." He took out the book and placed it on the table.

"But what do you mean by that?" Mrs. G. leaned her head on his shoulder. She laughed while looking through the pages. "Hitler believes in mystical things like this book entertains?" She skimmed the chapter titles.

"Yes, of course."

Marie said it was revolting to watch. "He takes ideas from any book that suits him, then twists them to his desire. For instance, this book matter-of-factly states the author's belief in original root races and that as time advances certain ones are left behind, just as old ideas are outdated. So do root races."

"Well?" Mrs. G. leaned towards his lips.

"You, my dear, of course, are of the superior race to be advanced further." He kissed her lips. "The pure Aryan race is the best. Of course, Hitler hides that he is part Jewish. He is against the Jews for different reasons. Mostly, he is frightened of their genius, their talents, gifts, and amazing ability to make money."

"That isn't a reason to be against them," Mrs. G. said.

The fifth root race will bring a higher renaissance of art, culture, and education, which he believes only the finest German blood can develop. He has a dream, only many of us suspect it won't happen the way he plans it, through destruction. He would shoot me if he heard me say this."

"Ah. So is that why he eats only vegetarian meals?"

"Of course. This book says that eating meat holds you to your lower self and takes from your abilities to think clearly."

Mrs. G. choked on her wine. She put her starched linen napkin to her face. Marie was sure she was laughing again.

The German answered that she and he will be part of the advanced humans. He touched her hand. "My boat is waiting if Hitler fails to conquer your country."

"Where do we go then?" Mrs. G. looked towards the hall, which led to the room of gold.

He leaned into her and said, loud enough for Marie to hear,

"We go elsewhere, my dear. Everything is in place. We take the gold, and flee. There will be another room in a different country to store it."

Mrs. G. said she first wants an airplane for herself.

The officer looked startled and said the sea is safer. He poured himself more wine and described how Hitler is counting on America being an ally, once Europe comes under German rule. "America does not wish to get involved in a distant war and repeat the First World War. America has it own problems. They do not suspect we are going to infiltrate them in a much different way, not by air, boats, but by violence within its very fabric. We have to eradicate the inferior races here, just as in Europe."

Mrs. G. ate a piece of sharp cheese made by the cook. She gulped down a quarter of her wine. She asked if there were any motives that would lead Hitler back to a plan for peace. Marie shivered then; she was not keeping calm. The cook in the kitchen pulled Marie back and gave her hot cocoa at the table by the window overlooking the back yard. As Marie stared into the darkness, a figure slipped from the woods and entered the shed door. He held a heavy box—more gold. Marie sighed.

The officer left the sand and stones beneath his symbol and photograph. He said something in German. Next morning, Marie had him write it down for her. She showed it to me: *"Es ist aber schoen"*—It is beautiful, though.

This is all I can write to you tonight, my Dawn. Greetings to my family. In my letters to them, I still only tell them what I do each day: chopping wood, mending wharves and sleeping at night at Grumble's. Tomorrow I am going fishing with some of the island boys. They are younger than I. It will be fun. We're taking the large rowboat out beyond the cove.

Affect'ly,
Cousin Fred

I held this letter as I sat on my rock. I carried each letter everywhere; then I placed it in the bucket. I trusted no one to them. I tried not to worry for him. I worked to let that go. He had adventure and happiness, if he only knew it.

CB CA

I can lie here now, close my eyes. Somehow, a memory like this makes me think I am young, beautiful. I almost get up and run outside. But I remain in my bed. I see nature is changing to deep summer flower: black-eyed Susans, Queen Anne's lace rim the shore. Frogs croak in marshes set in from the river. Yet a few peepers resonate from a swamp.

Think back on a river. Every word, thought flows past. You can put them into the water, new ones arrive.

I sat in the river shallows; I was deciding about a painting to begin. I wanted to take part of the beauty of this river, my rock, and inscribe it into time, where I could view it from a distant perspective. I wanted to express a transcendent landscape. "Beauty is eternal," Mam said. She'd ruffled my hair before braiding it. She pointed to light across the ridge above the river. Tossing the braid behind my back, I ran out into the meadow.

I have little pain, and when it comes, making me gasp, I have pain medicine given to me. Close my eyes again, and the sweet face of Mam comes.

Mam told me how during the plague people in France who were dying lay in front of paintings in a monastery. They gazed on colors and scenes which depicted suffering. Within the artist's rendition of religious events, something eternal shined in his paintings. He, the artist, painted a great healer, Jesus, suffering his final agony, showing his eyes looking on a heavenly sky.

Because Mam as a nurse worked with very ill patients, I knew she spoke from her belief that spirit could win over the body; an elevated matter might lift above a darker force. A face can shine at the threshold of death. In that second a person rises above the pain. Pain is density; it lodges in matter, is a voice of its own telling about illness, which is clamped down keeping people bound to matter. I asked: how did she stand constantly working with sick people? She only shook her head. She said it was hard to explain.

Out on the island, the employer of Fred, by his descriptions of her, was tied to matter; I wondered, would such greed lead to illness in her? No, it would not, but I didn't know that then. It seems only to have given her freedom eventually. She used the man who brought gold to her and who hung his photo on her dining-room wall, took fuel from her. And our village had dynamited two Nazis out of our existence. Both these kinds of actions were done out of a conviction of there being some truth that went beyond politics, wars. If only for a while, this employer knew she had only one chance to get off an island. Newspapers didn't reach islands then. Gold and a dream of wealth did.

The newspapers in our village came each day. They began to carry articles on Nazis possibly killing people for religion, race, and physical defects. These reports were rare because news filters through many sieves, Uncle said. Thousands of miles lay between Europe and us.

Placing my foot in the cold water, I wondered if I should shred the letter or not. Watch the pieces go down the river, tell Fred to deal with his world without me. Let me be in peace to paint, to mingle with memories of Mam. What a place I wanted! The ideal valley, community, me able to work at what I loved. Quite different, the history of my village.

Just up the road, a farm help had killed the farmer who employed him. This farmer was skinned and cut by him into pieces, put in a burlap bag, to float down the same river where I sat. For many years, he was in jail. I realized my village was not perfect, even before the Nazis.

CȜ   CȜ

Many people crowded around Mr. B.'s radio, discussing nothing but most recent political news. I rounded the corner where Mrs. B. sat, nearly colliding with her. One free hand gestured to me. She had a very extensive list, double the number of planes. Everyone with binoculars now had time to view air traffic. The question was, where are planes going? At which airports might they land? So far, they weren't enemy aircraft; Mrs. B. seemed sure of that. I breathed a deep sigh of relief.

"War is war," by that she meant war is serious, but the day means business as usual. Set had up the counter with items to tempt customers, while they listen to the news. Make some money off commotion. War is good for business. Her baked goods, especially the donuts, went before anything else except for the newspapers. Then there were the letters that came in. My, she knew everyone's family.

She handed out the mail, asked me when was the last time I picked up a letter from Fred. She was so sure that war would claim us some way or other.

Mr. B. heard that remark. He came over to see her airplane list. He shook his head, saying it sure is claiming his wife. He suggested we have ice cream.

Mrs. B. waddled from the mail section into the general store and demanded a cold ginger beer, along with an ice-cream cone.

Mr. B. hopped to the counter, said, "Sure, have one." He sat with her beside the cold woodstove. As they sipped cold drinks, they stared into a space behind the stove. I wondered what they were seeing. No spiders there, not even a cat; I almost blushed to find them holding hands, as they had been married since before World War I.

"Has your store changed since the old days?" I asked Mrs. B.

"Not much, dear. There's more modern things come along. We don't have to cut ice chunks out of the river and cover them with sawdust all summer. You'd think there'd never be anything different than the river providing us with ice. Land sakes, that changed and thank goodness. Sure, the newspapers change. But war is back. We always have war."

"Still have the chess games," said Mr. B.

"We have them," said Mrs. B. I thought how this store was more than a functional grocery provider. It was also a place of memories for the village. Each night, impromptu chess games got played here. When it snowed, Mr. B. let anyone come by to get warm by the stove. Door was unlocked. He and Mrs. B. slept in a room off the store, if they needed to discuss events all night, for instance, the recent village house bombing.

"What's Fred up to?" Mr. B. asked. He moved over to the counter.

I decided to tell him. "If you promise not to tell anyone, I'll let you know what he is doing."

Mr. B. solemnly nodded.

"Then I'll tell you. I am worried for him." I related most of the contents of Fred's letters to them both.

Mr. B. dropped his soda on the floor. Mrs. B. screeched and said that we best tell the government.

"When we told the government about our Nazis in this village, they did nothing," replied Mr. B.

"Do you think Fred is safe?" I asked Mrs. B.

Mr. B. raised his eyebrows, let them down again. His eyes got cloudy. I thought he had gone numb.

In winter, you hear the woodstove crackle in such silence. In summer, nothing but the bark of a dog. Dust floating in a sunray come down to the store. I picked dust out of the air, on purpose, in order to stall with Mr. and Mrs. B.

A fly buzzed, flailing wildly, caught by a spider in the high beams of the ceiling; the web rocked, the fly sounded like a machine, and finally Mr. B. coughed. The fly made more dust fall.

"Keep me informed. He's a lad who runs into trouble." He pointed upwards at all the spider webs hanging in angles.

"Can we get him out, Mr. B.?" I was thinking Fred would never return to be a farmer. He would never find contentment in watching his cows in the field.

"I think it's best to leave him on the island. He's in danger, any way you see it."

I gasped. That wasn't an answer to help the situation; it left me with no solution, alone, as if I were leaving him, separating his adventure from my own.

"And, Dawn, you can't do a thing. If you think anyone of us can boat into that remote place unseen—nope, it can't be done."

Mrs. B. said, "We must raise this frustration into God's hands."

The spiderwebs in the door caught the sun when she said that. I could see flies stuck there, too. Mam said thoughts in the invisible realm are intellectually alive. Every thought has a force or a being behind it, whether it is good or bad.

"Does he have a gun?" Mr. B. shifted his position and leaned on the counter.

"He has use of one where he lives with an old man," I said.

At that Mr. B. dusted the counter with the cotton rag. Mrs. B. washed that rag out by hand each night. Sometimes I helped her pick up the store, watching her do the basic routines. He hung the rag over the counter's edge. Sat down, picked up his pipe, knocked it out, then filled it back up with tobacco. His tobacco pouch hung on the shelf behind the counter. This was his way of getting out of talking. He left me alone with his wife.

"Fortunate you are only his cousin, not his sweetheart. Lizzie's been in here every day weeping over him, until I tell her, "Just dry your eyes and look to your ma and help her. Lizzie has a pretty face and looks that any young man will run after, soon as she gets over Fred."

I thought Lizzie was firmly set on Fred. She refused other boys of the village who come to the dances. With her smile and red cheeks, tidy figure, she could dance with ease; yet she let anyone know it was only Fred she liked. She studied English and wished to help run the village library, as the present librarian hoped to retire.

"You can tell a cousin a few things in confidence." I said. I wasn't sharing with her that Fred liked another girl now.

I took a peach from the basket, gave Mrs. B. a penny for it, thanked her for her kindness in sharing my burden.

"You need to share them with the Lord, my girl."

I assured her I would, possibly even sit with her in her pew. She exclaimed how closely I resembled my mother. Was I going into nursing too?

I shrugged. Maybe I would, but I had to learn to paint.

She must have taken that shrug for ambivalence. I must be a lost soul needing guidance at the very moment. She shifted on her chair, drew out a cigarette, lit it, and said nursing was a good profession. "There are not many people, let alone women, making a living at painting."

I told her she was right, but didn't I have my own home and a job helping Aunt Grace?

I ate the peach, walked across the bridge, and climbed the hill up to the farm.

Dear Cousin Dawn,

I told you we were taking out the large rowboat. A terrible thing happened. A fellow drowned. He fell out of the boat and sank because he couldn't swim. No one on the island knows how to swim. Can you imagine this? They say there's no point to it because the water gets you numb in three minutes, and then you are frozen.

We boys had to figure a way to get him from the bottom of the cove. It wasn't more than thirty feet from the cliffs, and high tide would come in and wash the poor fellow out to sea. Then someone had an idea. He took a harpoon with a rope attached to it. He threw it down into the water, and it went through the fellow's chest. They pulled him up on the rope. They couldn't get the spear out of his chest, and left it.

His ma was wailing, and everyone came running. They wrapped him in a blanket, took him up to his house to prepare the mourning. A man pulled out the spear. It was to be a closed-casket wake.

He is gone, but where to? I don't ask these questions too much, but seeing him living, jumping, excited in the boat, and next moment seeing him splash in the water with such a frightened look is enough to send me to a god, Dawn.

The wake will last a couple days, and then the funeral service is in the little church here, then he will be buried in the hillside cemetery, surrounded by thick stone walls and an iron gate.

Old Grumble on hearing my story said, "You pay respect to the dead, and then you get on with the living," We were sitting by the fire tonight in his cabin before I took up pen and paper to write you. I will write you until I am near falling asleep. I am still sleeping on the bench.

I haven't seen Marie and Yvette for a few days. I am waiting until the officer leaves. The mist and low fog roll in at night, hiding him and his rower as they go out to the U-boat to check it. They both still stay at the Big House. Yvette has a motherly fondness for him, despite his comments about France. He praises her cooking. He only speaks in German. She talks back to him in French, piecing together these languages over food. I peek in the windows at night to watch them dancing to records. The Germans are not bad at their steps. I prefer our village dances, Dawn. It is live music, and although it is different from this modern stuff, I like it better. Don't know why. Guess I don't feel comfortable with women in makeup, high heels, and low-necked blouses showing their bosoms to these men. I chide Marie because she joins them, but she laughs and says if I were just a woman, I'd understand.

Mrs. G. wears fancy dresses, and they are usually green, setting off her red hair. Marie says she wears makeup constantly now, much more than when I first arrived on the island. It isn't for me, Marie laughs.

She says, "The Nazi is Mrs. G.'s only contact with the world. At least, Marie dismisses my fears and says the Germans are much better to have around as spies than the Russians. I ask her what books she's been reading, and again she only laughs.

The officer, she says, tells her that America will surely be taken over by Germans or Japan some day and that those two countries are in league together, although in the newspaper you never hear about that. "The Russians are nothing," he spit on the floor.

He tells Marie never to worry. Her family and she will be looked after. Marie tells him that he is insane, but he says no to that, and underneath the sea is a whole world of spies travelling in their U-boats, sharing codes and secrets that no one can find out.

"And how do you get messages from one submarine to another?" Marie told me she laughed while asking him. He had an answer for that, only Marie wouldn't tell me. She is afraid of this man, even though she scoffs at him to his face. She thinks he wishes to impress her. Marie is very sophisticated looking, despite living on a Maine island.

Anger filled me as I read this description of Marie; I let the letter fall to the floor. Was Fred becoming a chaser of skirts? Then hastily I retrieved the letter, for someone would pick it up. Placing it safe under a book, I had to start my day, trying to get the thought of Marie out of my mind. I felt angry that my cousin was doing nothing about his life.

Morning clouds over the mountain, I dressed, combed my hair with my fingers. Wearing a print dress with an apron, I went down to the kitchen to start the stove, and breakfast—my daily job. After that, I had to milk Fred's cows. Then, I would brush them today and make their coats shine before putting them out to pasture.

When I'd forgot Fred's romantic feelings towards Marie, I pulled his letter out of my pocket again, walked down the hill to the store, stopped at the rock to continue it.

I have stayed away from the Big House for three days. I am cutting wood on the other side of the island. I visit the professor when I finish my work, and we play chess. He knows about the Nazi officer, because I wanted someone to be informed of the situation, aside from Marie and me. He is keeping this news quiet. He told me to stay within my bounds. Do my job, and stay clear of the Nazi.

The professor also told me that the Nazis study occultism, and the twist they make on Madame Blavatsky is that her theories of root races, which go through evolutionary phases, are behind the killing of Gypsies, Russians, and Jews and many more people. We hardly know about racial issues here in Maine, he says. We just had so-called witches in New England, who were hung in Boston long ago.

As he moved his chess pieces, he drank coffee and looked out to sea.

"It is also the Russians they view as an inferior race. The Germans wish to subjugate the Russians and make an alliance with America and then carefully control us. The cunning of Hitler only goes by maps and ideas, not reality," the professor said. He moved another chessman.

He says he was once the favorite of the Big House, when he first bought a house here. He was invited to meals; they conversed about poetry and philosophy. That was Mrs. G.'s intellectual era, he said. Now he shakes his head over her, saying, "The world seems all about money." I never got lost on that idea, because you can't eat gold and silver. He walked to the cabin with me and helped carry my heavy axes back. He asked Grumble to drive the professor's old car off the cliff.

Grumble roused himself from watching the fire, cursed, then saw a twenty dollar bill in the professor's hand. He said, "All right, Doc."

I gasped. Was the professor paying him to die? And just when he was saying the world was all about money, he pulls a wad of it out of his pocket. I guess, however, he doesn't have as much as this Nazi. Mrs. G. would be courting him still, if he had great wealth.

The next day was busy: I had two days off work to attend the wake and funeral. I used the time off also to sharpen the axes and stack wood for Old Grumble. Remember how you spoke, Dawn, of the Universal Spirit being the same as God and the angels being close to people? They have transcended to where their spirits are pure in the Universal Space, called Heaven? You say that people can become angels eventually. Your mam taught you these many things. You told me that sometimes you go to our church to be part of the good intentions and thoughts. Strong ideas strengthen the week ahead of one, you tell me. I will go then, Dawn.

I think I understand these things a little better out here. I've learned that whatever Mrs. G. does, the islanders shrug their shoulders. They don't care. The professor says people have free will to decide to be evil, or good. The islanders look evil in the eye. Let the Nazi do what he wants. The sea will be the judge. Takes people down in storms.

The professor says the islanders don't do what our village does, like blowing up a house or taking on a mission to make things better. On the island we are far out at sea, and everyone has to mind their own business. I don't think our Nazis counted on such a village as ours being in everyone's affairs. No bad could come to our village, Dawn. Just maybe I can get off this island alive to see you again.

If anything, the islanders love a story. So they aren't going to stop this saga of the Nazi. For instance, the baker Berta sent the Nazi officer freshly baked buns because she said he's a hungry man, and that strange uniform of his—she hoots over it. He has started walking down into the village from the Big House, dressed in his medals—doesn't mean he's less a man, Berta says. She sent Jimmy, her errand boy, to take them to him. The next day, the officer was in her little bakery, sipping coffee.

No one cares about politics out here. They want a way to earn their living. Up at 4 a.m. to go for lobsters, and home to eat and sleep.

The drowning brought this life to a standstill for a few days. Lobster boats stayed home. Even seagulls cried, Berta said, as I sipped coffee in her cafe. His brother and sisters walked beside his casket. The schoolteacher read an essay he wrote last year about the island that raised him and the sea that provided an income. That is all he came into life to do, he had written. It was this simple for him, and he didn't understand how others worried about what they should do in life. It is usually right in front of your nose, he wrote.

Not knowing him well, I took off my hat and stood at the door. The essay had moved me to think on my life and you all in our village. His mother turned her head to me and then put her handkerchief back to her nose. I'm a stranger here, yet this was a welcoming of me into their midst. Grief is communal, Dawn. I could see this great sadness.

After the funeral, Old Grumble drove the professor's car over the cliff. He hopped out at the edge and let it sail over. The professor and I crept to the edge of the cliff to look down at the smashed heap of old metal. He hoped tides would take it out to sea.

I went to stand by the graveside where the poor fellow was buried in the earth. I thought about how his life he loved was over. This is enough writing for now. I feel quite dismal and have to hike over the island tomorrow. The walk will cheer me.

Your cousin,
Fred

I placed the letter back in its envelope. I was relieved that he was getting familiar with the island village and not bringing me more strange news of the happenings at the Big House.

I then sat with Mrs. B. eating ice cream and swatting flies. I watched a customer buy flowers that I brought from Mam's garden. Since we were on a main road, everyone stopped at the store. It was a good way to sell my merchandise.

I think back to Mam working in her garden, and how she said to pick your thoughts. The ones you like are flowers. Stick to these ones. It isn't hard to find your life. Do what makes you happy.

She tended her roses, told me not to ignore the sense of smell. Put it into everything you do, because every creation that's founded with a dream has an aroma to it. "My job, Dawn, I love it, working as a nurse. The smell of it?" She laughed. "Like the earth turning over in autumn."

What Mam said stuck in my memory. Without these conversations, my memory would be empty, I thought. Sometimes I didn't understand everything she discussed, but after she died I seemed to get what she'd told me. I think I put off until I would be older to reflect on her words, thinking we'd have many more discussions.

A butterfly drifts onto flowers; Mam walks by. She turns to me; she is standing before the edge of a field. I think I smile, as I turn on my pillow.

ᘓ   ᘒ

As I set plants out by the store porch, a stranger came to talk. He asked me if Fred was my relative, and I muttered yes. I wanted to add he had left us. Went into dreadful situations. I bit my tongue, withheld further talk of my cousin.

"I'm not passing the time of day, Miss. Word is out that he is going to need some help, so I'm heading out to the island. I'll be watching him. I've got a gun."

"And who are you?" I asked. I was suspicious of strangers, and so was Mrs. B. She was sniffing the air like a dog. It wasn't a good smell, I could tell. She coughed.

Then another customer came over to me with two dollars and a request for a basket of salad greens and herbs. I excused myself from the stranger. Mrs. B. trailed me saying, "Don't you say anything more to him. He wishes to see how much you know. He's another Nazi, as sure as I can hear the accent on his tongue." I had heard it, as a matter of fact, but dismissed it. I don't know why.

I went back to eating my cone along the porch steps and told the stranger I had no idea what he meant. Fred writes he's having a wicked good summer and work is going well. Why, I didn't even know which one of the thousand islands he was even on.

The man left, staring into the distance with glazed eyes. He ran his fingers through his hair and shook his head. He went to the corner of the road to wait at the bus stop. The bus came, rumbling thunder. I watched him board, and the bus left, backfiring sparks from its muffler. Then I gathered my produce together for Mr. B. to sell inside the store.

Starting up the hill, I thought how well the summer was going; I was earning three dollars a week. My painting studio was almost ready. I had ordered supplies from a large mail order catalogue from Philadelphia. Each week, brushes, paint, or paper arrived. I then organized this equipment in the back room off the kitchen. The time was coming to start, and I needed to sit on the river rock and think. The painting would be a dark sky against green, the shadow as the stranger who had entered my herbs and flowers.

We were on the rock; Matt put his arm around me. "Only a friend," he grinned. Light lips, brushing my forehead, hardly there. I thought he did not want anything. Repeatedly I'd told him I wasn't doing anything like becoming his girlfriend. If he wanted one, there were plenty of girls in the village.

Today on the rock as he held me, we swished our feet together in the river; fish leapt at our toes. Sun slanted on the riverbank. Wild ducks shuffled in the shore reeds, while swallows caught flies.

It didn't seem that war could be raging overseas. Not on a day like this. With our Nazis gone, peace here was back, fragile, but it slowly settled. Such things shook it as the stranger confronting me about Fred. Mrs. B. had cautioned me just in time before I had described Fred being in danger.

I reflected that the islanders where Fred lived knew the officer was foreign, yet they weren't interested in his politics, because they weren't concerned about the political events of our country nor of the distant ones over the ocean. Their life was with only one foot on land, Fred had said. The waves took most things away.

Matt asked what were my thoughts. I said: none. I had let them go past the shallow side. I pointed downriver. He said he'd go with me to where I went in my mind. My brow tensed, and I searched for a place on the horizon he couldn't see, to run and hide.

"When you love someone," he said, "you walk with them, up and down river, even against the current."

I shifted position on the rock. He had never said, "When you love someone."

"Do you know that someone is you?" He turned his head to touch my cheek, and nestled his nose in my hair.

"Not sure, Matt." I am sure this is what Pa felt towards Mam, but he'd lost her. For me, to love meant heartbreak, worse than Nazis in our village. Nazis are temporary. Hurt that will go away. Rationally, we are the main route to Canada. I can see Canada from Uncle's farm. When the slaves were running for freedom, did they arrive in our village? Oh, yes.

And in the town where Gran lived, they were hidden in dirt cellars, if they feared pursuit, then taken at night to the borderland, so close to us.

Nazis are hardly mentioned in our newspapers, so I feel they're but a wind passing by, stirring dust until what is broken is forgotten. The house that was bombed scarred the landscape and puzzled me. Violence fled from the very intimate speaking of two people to each other of this word, love. Love was not something I thought about, and here was Matt, saying it.

That word rippled over the low rocks, sent out foam in currents, which whirled, then shot out into coves. The ducks garbled, picking their way awkwardly over pebbles until they found deeper water in which to swim.

Matt said, "Love you this high." His hand measured three feet. His voice died, where he went in memory; I walked with him where I could see him riding his pony across this part of the river into the fields to our home. Mam had cold cider for him to drink on a summer day. He lifted me onto his pony.

I didn't want to delve into my most intimate feelings. I liked to run from their pain. Mam and I had talked so often about stories, books, ideas, art, that if she had asked how I felt, I'd have said back then that I loved her and Pa. I was happy. She didn't ever have to ask me that, but I told her anyway. My love for my world was perfect. I did not ask myself back then: How could our souls ever die, if we leave this beautiful life? You don't disappear from your soul; I know this, at the end of my life. You merely pick up your skirts and traipse into another place, a star dome.

The Great Depression had lifted so slowly, like turtles coming out of river mud. Hope smelled like spring grass, wet fir needles. Mam and Pa had their farm paid for, and their work was secure. "Help others," she said. "You'll never be without a job." I lived within this security; I felt it alive in my body, a comfort even at night. After each day, I breathed deeply into sleep. Now, that bliss was gone.

I held Matt's hand more tightly. What if Mam were beside him, saying in his ear, "Be with my Dawn." How was I to judge this bending of fate, as birches in winter bend with snow? I gazed in the river and felt its force entreat me: just love. The fact was, I loved only a few people. They were safe, still part of my childhood. This would never change, I knew. They were Mam in Heaven, roaming Pa, Auntie, my Gram, no doubt searching for Mam in Heaven, and Fred. Matt was trying to enter the inclusive circle in which I existed.

"Someday I will love you, Matt," I whispered. I didn't say that I knew life would either help us or part us. That we needed to build a bridge to it. When terror hits your village, you keep what you love. "If I lose you, it is because I can't fit into what you want to do, or I can't fit you into what I need to do."

His head was resting on my shoulder. "Sitting here with you, let's not worry. What comes will come."

I pulled away, darting a look at him, as if he were about to fly. He was becoming wise at an early age, I thought, as I glanced at the sun shining on wisps of hair over his ear.

I let my feet touch a fish, which nudged against the weeds. I might reach down and scoop it up in my hands. Fish are abundant in these parts of the river. Dragonflies hang over the sand; gnats dance in the air. A bald eagle, swooping above the field, plunges to snatch a rabbit.

Matt watched the fish, held his finger out for a dragonfly. It fluttered away, having caught a midge. He watched it until water rushed in our thoughts, and we were empty.

"Will you marry me, Dawn?" He turned to me. If I'd felt his words echo on the shore twenty feet away, then the wind could have touched my lips. The eagle landed on the fir tree and stared ahead.

He was persistent; I give him that. I heard the answer inside me first. I looked at Mam walking along the shore. She nodded: "Oh yes, go ahead and do that, Dawn. It is the beginning. Not the end."

"Sure, Mam?" I asked her.

"More than ever," she said.

I said those words, "I will."

We didn't touch. God said, "Let there be light." Creation did its business; there was no smooching until things settled down with the bustle of a new world.

I picked up a stone and watched it jump across a smooth river cove at a distance from the rippling shallows.

ᙍ   ᙏ

Matt washed his cows until they shone then drove them into their fields with his chants, O-ah, O-ah! It was as if they laughed, with their tails swishing off flies. I walked with them and him in the mornings, following tails. The morning had a smell of Lady's Breath flowers of New England; I picked them for Aunt's home. I didn't tell her of our engagement. We could spend our life engaged, I figured. What did we know of the future? We had to walk in the day that for a time fitted into place.

"Such a wind!" Matt inhaled the air.

I thought it's a wind where you tell the heat of the day by the color of the hills. Hazy oscillating blue—heat is due.

He said, "Going to be a hot one. I'll pick daisies for Ma, and you both can put them into some pretty vases." He took off his flannel shirt, the one from the small L.L.Bean store in a village south of us. We picked shirts of flowers. His dog nipped a cow's back leg to keep it moving.

"Don't be rough on the cows!" Matt caught his dog by its tail. We were on the open side of the meadow, which looked out over the mountains. Good crop of apples this year, I noted, looking at the thick-leafed apple trees along the road. Blossoms had been substantial in the spring.

I marveled at his exhilaration. He bent down to touch the earth. Pulled daises up by their roots, such a hurry to please me. The earth smelled damp.

"Come see my ma at our house, and we'll get your little home fixed into the best art studio you've ever imagined." He held my hand to his chest's deep inhalation.

I smiled then. I had no regrets saying "I will." I know Mam saw into my heart and mind. She knew I was jumping into my life, my village, my painting.

Matt helped me in this; I had no expectation our life would be peace. It was for a while, but I mustn't jump ahead. That it had to be this way, so I could know who I was—I at sixteen and he twenty-two.

"It is our mind which centers matter," Mam said one winter. She was profound in conversations looking on the white of fields, when snow covered the dark earth.

We drew patterns on matter. We used cloth to make a quilt. "Age is endless: when you find the right moment for planting your age in ground, seize it."

She traced a design onto fabric to lay in the giant square. It was a small quilt for a child in the hospital where she worked.

Tears drop like moonstones. I have a moonstone ring. It is Mam's. I wear it even now. It reminds me to close my eyes again, remember everything. Matt and I started to his ma's, but I kept thinking to milk Fred's cows by late afternoon. The two farms were near each other, down the lane. My hair blew and caught in a berry bush. Thorns tangled in each strand.

Matt let the cows lope; the dog pushed them with his nose against their flanks. I watched them scurrying with his barks. My state was futile to resist, for if I pulled forward, the branch scraped skin. I was stuck. Matt took each strand of hair, untangling it. We watched the branch flip up to the sky. Then he lifted me from the thicket and placed me hidden down in the grass. As he entered me, I pictured mud roads and the peepers' first song; the nighthawk darted into a fir tree. What screeching it made as I burst and I screamed. A dead bird lay on the ground right beside Matt. Take that away, Lord, take it away! Don't let that be for us.

"He cannot, little Dawn," Mam answered from way out by the trees blown.

"I don't believe in predestination, Mam," I screamed.

"Don't have to, darling. Your life is written in your hands, forehead, eyes. 'Patterns,' they call it."

Dear Cousin Dawn,

Matt wrote me you were married in the church by Pastor Will. This is amazing news. I am not sure why you got married so fast, except Matt said you couldn't live in sin, according to my mother's admonishments. She found the cows went home untended, and mine weren't milked until morning, full udders they must have had, and you both found sleeping under a bush, almost bare naked. So, I guess if you love and are loved and forever wish to stay in love, being married isn't going to change that. It makes the village leave you alone. The talk will die down.

I love you, my cousin, and if you weren't my cousin, I'd have been your suitor, but God made us only as close as brother and sister. I wish I could ask it to be different, but it was preordained that we are family. Matt, my closest friend, deserves the best, and he has you. How does this happen overnight, for you were a slip of a girl, at least you seemed this to me when I left for the island.

You have hinted of so little in your letters. Yet, I believe you will find your way with someone, rather than to be alone, as you told me you desired no one with you in life. Your mother was so close to you, you didn't need anyone. But closeness, Dawn, to someone invisible, has no physical warmth. You maybe feel this now when Matt puts his arms about you. I have lost no one close, as you have. Yet, I have lost such things as a cow, milked her for years and held her through any pain she had, and when she went, I walked as though numb. Walked through the fields, over rocks I climbed. I could still hear her crying, even though she was dead, and I was still searching for her calf.

You had me close for years, especially after your mam died. I am so sorry I had to leave you. However, I am happy for you. You and Matt are my best friends. I can say anything to you, and you understand me. I wish I could settle down early, but my energies are high. I will have to be older when I am ready to settle back and read. Best to do what you wish when you are young: it is the only way. So, I envy you. Matt wrote your wedding was very small, attended only by my folks, sister and brother and Lizzie.

The day was perfect and you were beautiful, Matt said. You wore your mam's wedding dress. If only she could see you, how you have a home again, a place to carry on many things that your mam wished to do herself.

Will you be living in your old house or going to Matt and his ma's place? Whatever you decide, know I'll be back to see you one day. Then we'll also carve a design in the gravestone for your mam and make where she's buried a place where you can find your thoughts and hers together. We haven't talked about this since after she died, but you know I haven't forgotten how you love peace, in contrast to my fascination with danger. Thinking of you and Matt, there is a slight mist staring around the cove at me, nudging me to sleep. I will finish this letter, put sleep in the outhouse.

Winds have been rough. Too choppy to take out the rowboat. She and I would be smashed against the piers. She's a darling of a boat, but the tide is unusually high. I walk the beach at low tide thinking of my little sister and Jeremy, how they'd like to pick the beach of what's left, as we dump-pick at home.

About the Nazis on the island here: the German officer has left, but Marie says he'll be back. I am going to the Big House to deliver groceries and mail to Mrs. G. and to take the mail to the post office. The weather is stormy. We haven't seen the sun for a few days. Fog comes over the shore and sits on the fields. I bring wood into the shed, stacking it in cords.

On most days, when the Nazi is here, he and Mrs. G. watch me work. They ride on horses, holding the reins tightly. Mrs. G. has the crop ready to flick the horse, so I know she doesn't want to stay long to talk. He says I work well and tells me I need to court a young woman. He constantly wears his uniform. Marie says it saves on doing his laundry, and at night he sleeps in nothing. When I ask her how she knows that fact, she grins and says Mrs. G. washes his underwear.

The German stumbles with his accent. The horse backs up and nearly bumps into the stump of a tree I felled. I tell him, "I have to have a profession first before I have a lady." Mrs. G. laughs at that. "Just look at what's around you and where you can fit in," she says.

Marie listens to gossip at coffee time at the Big House, and she is frightened. She keeps her mouth shut most of the time. She continues with her employer, Mrs. G. I admire her courage, for I would rather go back to the mainland. Marie isn't glad that I wish to leave.

The U-boat has gone away. Temporarily, Marie says. We watched it load up on fuel from a long hose from the island fuel tank, set on a hill behind the houses by the harbor, where the boy drowned. I call it Black Harbor.

Marie says Mrs. G. gazes at the sea, her eyes intent on the horizon, as if a whale will spout. Maybe she misses the officer and the nights of dancing. Remembers the red wine and the hope he gives her. He looks hard at her when she wears a red dress. Marie speculates the officer will return with more gold.

Marie's brother is coming out to the island to visit her. His name is Jack, short for Jacques. And then, guess what? Mrs. G.'s niece will arrive here soon. Marie says we'll have enough people for record dances. The Nazi, Mrs. G., Marie and I, Jack and the niece. How about that? Don't tell Lizzie. Our village dances aren't in fashion anymore. You put on the records and crank the handle, because the electricity doesn't work out here most of the time. Jimmy will do that winding for us.

It's called swing dancing. Marie teaches the professor and me the steps. We practice on his porch on my lunch break. Then, we drink coffee and smoke. The professor says the reason the Nazis are in rural Maine is simple. They are spying. Of course, complexity will follow every simple plan.

They are taking extensive notes inland and a small bit on the island economy, based on small villages and agriculture still at the center of daily life. They are studying the *Völkische* movement and wanting to put it to practice in a place such as in Maine, where agriculture exists and industry has not destroyed this pure village structure, which the Nazis adore. They believe in a concept called the "peasant aristocracy." They find we have it here, and if they conquer this country, eventually, which indeed is their plan, boy, then maybe Maine will be truly its capital—Augusta, not Washington, DC. They want to wipe out some of the races of people, not only because they are not blond and tall, but also because they despise commerce, money being the only intent of commercial life.

Initially excited about this, I was fading out of this conversation fast. I got scared. The professor said unfortunately they believe in killing to achieve their ideal of return to 19th-century pre-industrialization. Extermination of peoples, for instance the Jewish people.

I said, "That isn't in the newspapers or on the radio; how did you learn it? The professor took a second cigarette from a pack on the chess table. He tapped the cigarette and offered me one. My hand was shaking, so he lit a match for me.

The professor said, "You may not wish to know this, yet you must. The Nazi officer comes here to play chess with me each day, and we talk as if we were fellow countrymen, because we converse in ideas. The island is not of much interest to him, except to load up on fuel and sleep with Mrs. G. Sex is an animal drive for the Nazi. He says he roars when he has it, not just out of pleasure, but he has the best ideas in the middle of the act. Like wine, it is a necessity."

I am making myself sick writing this, so I'll get back to Marie, who has learned to swing by watching the Nazi and Mrs. G. The Nazi's boy swings the cook around. You can see them from the window. She's big, and he is short, skinny. The island men are beginning to sneak to the Big House windows at night to watch the dancing. They go up, one at time, to view them at 8 p.m. It is going to interfere with their lobstering, their wives say.

You probably don't have time to read my long letters. Write me when you can. I love to read about your ideas for your paintings. I want to know how you raise money for your paints and paper. That is swell you figured that out. And how is Lizzie?

Your cousin Fred

A shoebox under my bed holds each letter from Fred. When the days get long, the nights brief, my white hair wisps like cirrus clouds. I am light in my mind, young as a baby. But as sure as apple pie, you get old. I have only to look at my skin hanging on my hands. So, it reminds me I am almost good to go—jump into my summer dress, the apron on my bedroom door, streaked with red juice from berry bushes. This fruit sold well at my stand.

My handwriting was large, hurried. I had to get a card off.

Dear Fred,

I've been berry picking. What kind of berries do you have out there? I don't have much time for a letter. My plants sell, so I can afford paints now. I hope you are being good. I can write a decent long letter at another time. Matt and I do just fine.

> Your cousin,
> Dawn

Another letter came swiftly.

Dear Cousin Dawn,

Good to hear you are berry picking. Your pa's berry patch is the best in the village. I am glad you are using it. Be sure you have my ma bake pies for your stand. You are an enterprising woman. It is good you are having success at selling. I think people come because they see your hair light up, and you have such sweet eyes that say kind things without any words needed. How many times do I tell you that?

Speaking of this, a stranger turned up on a boat and is living with the postmaster and his wife. He is visiting the island for a few weeks until the next ferry comes. That will be next month, actually. He came through the village and described you. He said you weren't the overly friendly type. I guessed you suspected him of being another Nazi, so I will be very careful, Dawn. Do not fear for me. I have fear, but that is not your worry.

Jack has come. He and I fish for mackerel off the town wharf. We take them back to Old Grumble, where the three of us feast. The stranger saw us fishing and asked if he could join us for dinner. I made an excuse; I forget what I said; my knees were shaking. Think I told how Old Grumble hates company and has a loaded gun. The stranger shrugged, walked over the boards, crunched his fine leather shoes on the dry seaweed.

When strangers observe everything we are doing, commenting on my repair of the docks or the way I throw the line into the water for fish, I expect there's no harm in being friendly. I won't impart any information to him. I know nothing, right? Don't even know about the house blowing up in our village.

You keep smiling, cousin. I was telling Jack about you and Matt being married and settling into two houses. Said you were found naked together, under a berry bush. We had a good laugh. You keep your spirits high, like mine.

Your cousin Fred

I am so young with Mam near me in the night realm. Always there to protect me, she slipped away by dawn. I remember having a deep distrust that Matt would disappear. I held back whenever he pulled me close to him. I knew a marriage was no marriage until it was consummated. What we did under the bush didn't count, Aunt said. The looks the village girls gave me the day after the wedding night—enough to make me hide in the barn. Yet I faced them enough to hold my head high and not feel badly that our marriage night had not gone as normal tradition says it should. Our friendship was strong, what we supported in each other.

After our wedding, we slept in the meadow. Stars appeared, and then sunrise came on the east ridge. Our sweaters over us, we woke with cowbells clanking. The milk cow sniffed my ears. I jumped, thinking I'd forgotten to milk her, but then Matt whispered that I had three days off work. I stroked the cow's face until her curiosity was gone, and she wandered off.

Matt whispered, "Do that to me."

I ran my hand down his face, across his fuzzy beard, over the rim of his ears. All the time I looked into his eyes.

He said, "We have a lifetime, I pray, girl, so that's all I ask for now—your gentle touch and look." He looked up to the barn, where Uncle stood in the door, surveying the day.

"That's what I like about you, Matt." I wondered if Uncle saw us.

"Time to discover love's domain," he yawned, bent over to braid my hair. "It'll take me years to tame this," he said, putting my hair around his head. "A new cap for my head," he said, pulling me over him.

I brushed off grass from my gingham dress, shook my hair loose from his hands, looked into the sky. Horsetail mist moved upriver; ducks flew out of a copse. Whatever fox pursued them was stopped by this protective depth of river. After honking, the ducks swam, fishing in the shallows.

Matt held my hand. "We should go skinny-dipping." I choked back my excitement. The morning hung over the river. I ran to the sandbank, threw off everything but my silk slip, which Aunt had made. I wasn't going to be seen naked again.

"Silk," she said, her voice trailing with her eyes out the window of the sewing room, "is as air when you wear it close to your skin. You are cool in summer, warm in winter." I hand washed my slip each evening, hanging it to dry in the window. Such a wind could come to shake it, if it could. By morning it was sleek, shimmering, gasping to be worn again. Peach colored, like skin, was my silk.

I looked away when Matt took off his clothes, as if the part of me shy of him in a meadow at night was also unable to see him beside rocks, water rippling. We found a deep pool, plunged in. Diving off a slippery rock, coming up out of water for breaths, and brown trout darted into murky crevices.

The last dive, and we went between rocks below water level. I saw the channel opening into darkness; there were caves under the rim, and in those caves were dirt, moss-covered nuggets of gold. Our river was known for this treasure, but the gold mine had closed down because they thought they could bleed the river dry of this gold. Yet, I knew where just a few more fist-size lumps lay. I was saving my knowledge, told to me by a Native American. Saving it for a time when Pa returned, an old man needing caring for. I'd be the one to tend to his dreams and send him to Heaven, but that is another story, not now.

Matt caught me before I was going to slither into the channel and pulled me back. Panting for breath, because I'd decided to hold it and go underneath for a while, checking on it, forgetting my husband. A thought that comes to you sometimes needs following, Mam would say.

"What's down there?" Matt asked me.

We had surfaced and pulled air into our lungs. "My cave," I whispered. "You can't tell."

He brushed the wet, hanging bangs from his eyes. "Then, it's best to keep it distant from me yet, my girl. Not to be explored. First, this."

He held me then, without scarcely my knowing it; softly his hands caressed my wet skin, and with him I blended with the river and left the fish to nibble our toes, without our feeling them. Under water, veiled, light currents moved, and then sunlight peered into the river cove.

 War

At the river rock, I put my legs into the water, with nothing to do but think—about life so far. Matt worked in the fields. My herb and flower business was growing. My land beside the river was perfect. I had only to touch the soil and plants arose, danced in gowns.

I grew the peaceful women, white-tipped chamomiles. Alongside them was lemon balm, the grandmother of sleep, leaves bending over. Furry sage smelled, enlivening tea with its scent. Elderflowers and linden blossoms came later on in summer. I dried them and then stored them in jars. The peaceful women soothed crying babies for weeks after birth. Mam used this herb, making it into tea. Stirred it until it cooled enough to feed the babies from a small spoon, even day-olds took it from her.

The local midwife who bought my herbs needed help in the winter months, and I said I'd first think on that during the summer and discuss it with Matt. Decide how that might fit into our plans. When I told Matt, he was for it. Said my mam was a nurse, seems like it's in my blood. He suggested I work eventually in the hospital like Mam. They'd fit me into it, hands-on, he said. I'd have my herbs in the summer, get them dried for the midwife, help her when she needed me, and have my painting as my hobby year-round. Mam had a side business. She made quilts.

I stepped from the rock, lifted my dress and waded through waist-deep water to the farthest shore, a shortcut to my house. I did well that day with plant sales. I even milked Fred's cows in the early morning. Now, I went home to paint.

I made a path through the grass to avoid walking on the bare ground; dry dust rose with each step. That way, arriving at the kitchen studio, I was damp with river-grass dew and fresh as morning flowers. The kitchen was bright, windows with screens in them. I sat at the easel to work on a landscape of our valley. It was as if I were the Creator, making a scene, envisioning it with perfect beauty. In the side meadow, at the end of it, I painted the farmhouse that had blown up.

I wanted to put it back and make the village and the surroundings idyllic, without the hole that remained where the Nazis had lived.

I painted undisturbed until a fly dashed against the window screen. It flew back into the kitchen; in the hall, the grandfather clock chimed. A bird called from the fir trees. It was not a bird, but Matt's imitation of one.

I went to stand by the window and watch my husband come through the grape arbor, bending his head under the vines. Opening the screen door and then letting it slam. He held me and muttered hello. I said that he smelled of sweet grass.

"Yes, we hayed a two-acre field today. Early this year, but rain is coming; lucky we got it in today. He put his fingers through my hair and reached up into my scalp, across my eyes, ears, neck, into my blouse, and I felt blood in my cheeks, already hot from the day. "You're beautiful, my Dawn." He kissed me until I gasped and pushed him away.

"Look what you've been working on," he said. "It's swell. It'll be for our grandchildren long after we are gone from this valley."

"Good you came, Matt. I'm done for the day. Want to race me to the river?"

His eyes lit up. "We'd better hurry. Ma has supper ready for us." He helped me wash brushes, put the paint away. We shut the door, ran to the water on the meadow path. Underneath the water, I saw the dark channel behind the rocks. I held my breath as long as possible, keeping my eyes open, then emerged gasping for air. I wondered how I could get back there. Matt held me sternly with his eyes.

"Not now," he said. "Promise me this. You could be lost down under there, and what would I do then, sweet Dawn?"

I wanted to reply to him but kept quiet—finding more river gold could wait. I did not need it. Mam said the Native people never asked the earth to give them her gifts unless they were desperate for help. I worried for Pa. Gone from me, but did I think he had needs?—he was fending for himself and didn't even write me. "I promise."

Rocks surrounded us diving into deep pools. Against the mountains, we were one wild spirit. Different from my brush on paper.

❦　❦

A letter came from Fred: Mr. B. held it up to make sure the envelope wasn't open. He said, "These thick envelopes must be fascinating reads. Wonder no one has tried opening the envelope." He handed it to me. The store was quiet in early day. Mrs. B. drank coffee. I sat on the barrel. We listened to the radio news of the war in Europe. A dog pushed open the screen door. Mr. B. went behind the counter to find a treat for the dog to chew.

"How's married life?" he cleared his throat. "I remember Mrs. B. and I. What a time it is, never forget it. You must have fun together before the work begins . . ." his voice trailed off. I knew they had seven children, and four of them died of scarlet fever when very young.

As if reading my thoughts, he muttered, "The three strongest children survived, and good sons they are to us. When they were babies, what a merry-go-round life was! Mrs. B. and I never had a moment to walk together, hold hands. We were just too tired and exhausted to . . ." He looked away again, decided to come back and finish his thought. "To have romance."

He cleared his voice, "Tell Matt my advice is to let his lovely wife dream and paint."

I lifted my head to watch the dog jump on the screen door to push it open again, ears flopping, tail high. Mrs. B., put down her coffee mug, held the binoculars, and took a pen out of her bun. "Child, you lost a great deal in one storm; chunk of sand leaving the riverbank, washed away your mama." She patted my head. I stood taller there.

Mr. B. let out a breath and then began wiping the counter, making it shine. His day could start. "Don't lose yourself, Dawn, to someone's life. Find your own happiness. Trust your heart. Follow a plan, but make sure your heart is in it."

I felt the full current over my rock. Rushes dipped in the water, rooted to the shore. Ducks strained with their wings to reach an eddy. I wanted to be in the river, not here at the store. I said, "Don't worry, Mr. B. I laid out a plan one night with Mam as we looked at the stars. If I follow what I like doing, I'm bound to be fine. She told me the universe sang a gorgeous song that night."

Mr. B. looked from the window to the corn-and-bean factory, where people filed in to work. They weren't doing corn canning yet; it was too early in the season. Soon it would be time for putting up vegetables, which took preparatory work. When canning time came round, anyone willing to scrape corncobs, cut beans, make jam, put labels on jars, had a job. With the war abroad, people saying we were getting into it, food rationing was starting. Hard times, people said, drove up prices. Food our village grew was a dear commodity. I was wondering if I should be settling down young or find a way to travel. He said, "Dawn, your mam struck out and did her own thing, yet came here, finally, to settle down. You'll take that last piece of her life, the settling, and do the same. I could urge you to strike out too, leave and find out about life away from the village, yet you'd be wondering about your herbs, plants, and your house. Your mam's heart is with you here now. Plus, your painting is an excellent endeavor, anchoring you to a discipline."

The factory whistle shrilled. Dogs howled at the noise. A cat scurried down the steps. I had to water the plants, put them out in front of the store. Mr. B. liked my business, for it brought customers to his store. "Back to work," he said. He wiped his hands on his apron and straightened his tie. His wife starched and ironed his shirts. He wore cufflinks and walked stiffly in the early day, until the starch wore off by afternoon. He stuffed his cufflinks in his pocket then.

"Fred will return, you wait and see," he said. "He's got your mam's side of the family—adventurous blood in him."

Mrs. B. sat rigid with the binoculars pointing to the sky. I looked up and saw the airplane with my own eyes. She hastily wrote the letters and numbers which were displayed on its belly. If it were an enemy plane, would we run inside our houses? There's no plan made for that, I mused.

Mrs. B. watched the plane fly westward, then put down the binoculars. She said she liked my plants today especially; they looked very healthy. "How do you do this?"

"I make manure tea for them, Mrs. B. They thrive on it. "I waited for her reply until it felt my cheeks were splitting red. Mam would not have me teasing like this. Yet, I did make this for them, out of water, manure and soil. You let it sit in a bucket for days, and then you spread it on the ground by each plant when the smell is thick and rotten.

"You don't say," said Mrs. B. as she cleaned her binoculars with her white lace handkerchief. The clouds were rising over the fields like white daisies brushing each other. "Bend over here," Mrs. B. said. "You've no Mam left, and your Auntie's asked me to talk to you. What will you do if a child is on the way? Takes over your life; hard to do all the things you do, or even paint."

She put her arm around my shoulders. The binoculars swung on her neck. She continued, "We've known you forever, Mr. B. and I. So don't mind us being like your parents sometimes."

I sat on the grass beside her chair. Wrapped my arms around my legs. "You know, Mrs. B., I don't mind. I earn my living with working for Aunt, selling herbs in summer, and I'm starting a winter job with the midwife. She told me how to follow the moon cycle and not have an unplanned pregnancy. Don't think I'm ready for a child. I'll be careful, don't worry.

Too much to do before I am a mother. Mam told me children were a comfort only in old age."

By the river, where we skinny-dipped, the moon didn't rise over the hills until midnight. I forgot to be cautious. A child was far from my thoughts. I glanced quickly at Mrs. B. to see if she was going to talk with me more about this subject, but she looked distracted.

She picked up her binoculars to observe a distant plane. Her frown increased, and the pencil scribbled some words, "Distant plane, too high up to see its numbers." Then she lowered her shoulders, placing the pencil down again. She sneezed as mist settled on a river bend. We watched rain move up the valley. She blew her nose.

"Your pa will be back. I can sense that. Don't give up remembering him."

I had nothing to say. He never wrote. Yet, the village never stopped talking about him.

 number number

I had stuffed the letter from Fred in my pocket and now opened it. I made my way to the river. Matt was in the upper meadow, haying. He promised to come for a swim and to sit with me on the river rock. I was keeping better track of the moon phase with my cycles.

When we swam, if it was the wrong time of month, I slipped away, out of his reach under water. All I had to do was to whisper, "I am going to the cave, dive under water," and Matt forgets everything else to chase me, for fear of me disappearing in currents. I kept remembering that we needed to be careful, as Mrs. B. said. Only I didn't tell Matt about her talk with me.

I remembered to use a rope when I explored the dark cave. I repeated constantly the directions: "Tie the rope to my leg; leave the end of it attached to a strong tree branch. Pull myself back out with the rope, if need be. I had maybe, a full minute to get to the chamber. That is what my Native American friend had told me.

Matt was walking upstream, staking out fishing pools. I went underwater and saw the fist-size nuggets. They were dirty and moss-covered. I held my breath for what seemed minutes, then surfaced, swimming back to the cove. In a half second I decided on three to take, put them in a leather bag on shore. I then climbed onto the rock, to my dry dress with Fred's letter safe in its pocket. That I explored underground caves needed never be told. I saw there was gold there, enough for my lifetime. The earth guarded this gold, keeping it safe. For some reason I took it; to this day I wonder about my "hunches," as Mam called this sense of something coming.

I had my life here; the river showed me its riches. I was glad it was not the angry river, carrying debris downstream. Spring, summer passed into August; tiger lilies bloom there always by the shore.

Dear Cousin Dawn,

I had a fever, which the islanders say came all the way from Germany. Many of us out here have it. Where else did it originate but from the German? Marie says the officer was sick in bed for two days after he got off the U-boat. Yvette, the cook, brought him tea and toast three times a day. She looks formal in her starched, white apron and hat. She ironed it for visiting his bedroom, to look proper, so afraid she was, Marie said.

In recovering, I am boring Grumble with my presence. I rest, doing nothing much to help him. Told him I'd carry in wood enough for the next two weeks as soon as I'm up. He shuffles about the room, keeping the fire going for me. It is damp and wet out here this week. Fog is thick. Heavy fir branches scrape the cabin wall. Am glad to be inside, quite honestly. Marie visits us to tell me news of the House.

The German officer is still away. The other stranger you spoke of also arrived here and is staying at the House. Marie doesn't like it because she has to serve the table, dress in a black-and-white outfit, and clean the room. I told her to figure out what he's doing here. It isn't unusual for strangers to come here and stay in the Big House. However, Mrs. G. takes in "high quality guests," as she calls them. They have to rank in something. In what? Perhaps, the German language? Marie says Mrs. G. believes it is a very sophisticated language. The stranger speaks with a German accent, not French because she knows that language and how the French sound when they speak English. Marie is certain the stranger is waiting for the Nazi to return.

Do you and Matt go to the barn dance each week? Are they still going on? Does Matt fiddle for them? How are you two doing? I want to know if you decided which house to live in. Marie shakes her head over you two. She says, people first married don't often have a house even. Look at you—I know I've said this to you before. How will you decide?

I haven't heard from Lizzie in a month. Has she found a new dance partner? You haven't written about her in your letters. It's okay to tell me if she's found another sweetheart. It'll hurt me some, but then I'm the one who left her, and I don't expect to return anytime soon. I don't blame her for being upset and finding solace in someone else's company. She knows how to run a household. I'm not the one she really wants.

Did I tell you Mrs. G.'s niece is here? How could I forget that? A replica of her aunt, only younger. How could God create two similar beasts? Bright orange hair, wild curls, fiery temper. Maybe I got sick because of her. The worry she creates just makes me nervous. Everywhere I go, she follows on her aunt's horse. Calls me boy! Thinks she has to check on me. "You taking a break now, boy? What for?" If she says that to me, I put down my axe, lean against a stone wall even more heavily, puff on two cigs instead of one. Get this, I hold a cigarette in each hand, take slow puffs and take a half-hour break, instead of fifteen minutes. Watch her until she gallops off. She is from Boston. She is only my age. She likes me, Marie says of her. Marie teases me, but I assure her, and you, that I'm not after that sort of woman. Out of my class entirely. I think the stranger likes her, and he's possibly fifteen years older than she. He follows her with his eyes, when she's inside the Big House, Marie says. You wait. She'll draw him to Boston next, away from the Nazi officer.

Rumors are the Nazi will return in less than two weeks. He went up the coast, maybe to hide gold in other people's houses.

Got to sleep now. Best to you and Matt.

Your cousin,
Fred

Days went on unhurriedly. I didn't try the rope again. I kept it under a bush by the river. I had no more plans to explore under the river. The words of my Native American friend came to me whenever I got tempted to take river gold: "Leave to the earth what is its treasure, unless you are in dire need." Their people go into the caves underwater when in need of food for the family, or if they have to buy a horse.

Matt was on his grandfather's farm, helping him get in hay, away for three days. That gave me time to paint.

It is odd I took three nuggets from the river, but I just knew I had to. I kept them under my bed—until the need comes; who knows when need comes? Mam would say, "Where your heart is—is your treasure, not in gold."

I completed my first large painting. Perhaps this was an ordinary achievement, if anyone who doesn't paint thinks about it, but for me a single landscape of our valley was the world mirroring my heart. The valley, river and rock will be one memory when I slide off to Eternity.

I had made small ones. Paintings are hard to let go; they cluster around. I had kept in mind that I needed to sell as many as possible. Thus, I worked hard until I felt able to release each one. The large painting, I displayed it alongside herbs and plants at the store. It stood out there. Someone would buy it.

Meanwhile I prepared the sketch for another canvas, depicting Uncle's meadow, where you see northern mountains. The horizon rests in heavily; a storm is due. Daisies blow in the foreground.

In the early morning, I put out my plants by the store. I placed my first painting there beside the sage and lavender. Many of the herbs got dried for winter use. The village women enjoyed fresh-cut flowers and mints for their teas, fresh lettuce, which I wrapped in damp cheesecloth.

A stranger stopped at the village store. We had an inordinate amount of traffic, being on the only good road. He was very tall, light-haired; he ignored my plants, going straight to my painting. He stood before it, then walked over to me and gave me twice the amount of what I was asking. "It is worth more to me because it is a picture of what I think of as Eternity," he said. "It is what I imagine an afterlife world to be." His accent was brisk, clipped, with trilled *r*'s.

I wondered what another foreigner was doing in our village. They come over the Canadian border because it is the best route south, Uncle had told me. "From where are you coming?" I asked.

"Straight down from Canada," he replied, bowing slightly to me. "I wish you much luck in more paintings. It is post-impressionist realism you do. Very vogue." His voice lowered. "I will put this on the wall of my home, and think of you." He looked into my eyes, and I looked wildly away.

Remembering my manners, I reluctantly glanced back at him, thanking him. I realized again that our small village store served as a respite for weary travelers. For my business's sake, that was fine. I had just sold my first painting. How wonderful! I graciously shook the hand he offered me, as if an Angel had visited our village, and then he turned and went away, my painting under his arm. He stood to wait for the next bus going south. I left quickly then, to return to my studio to paint.

I had called that painting *Hope*. It shimmered with yellow light cast on peaks, illuminating the valley. The river came from these mountains, tumbling down thousands of feet, winding through villages, and finally to the coast. I depicted morning because hope is quiet then, almost hidden. You can pass by it. You can stand in the mountain field and feel how its radiance enters day.

If I had put in one figure or house, it would have taken from its story. I left it unburdened with people and the works they construct. I let layers of paint dry and applied veils of color over each other. Gradually the painting resembled a mystical setting.

The studio had grown dark. I lit a lamp, took bread from the cupboard and cheese from the cloth, pumped water from the sink to make tea. I ate slowly and thought of Mam here, reading by this very lamp. Pa coming in from the barn to wash up and sit down to a late supper, if he'd had a long day of visiting farms and sick animals. The three of us would sit quietly, me sketching and watching the lamp flame. Words didn't seem to be necessary, as tiredness blocked all but the heart.

Pa stood up, put his arms around Mam, saying, "Bed and sleep, sweet." I wandered outside our house to catch the last shadow darkening across the field.

When I'd finished painting, I thought about the day, as I lay on my old bed, a light quilt pulled over me. Dark closed in. I leaned to blow out the lamp, heard the wind whistle through the window. Mam came through the wind to kiss my cheek and say, "I am not far away. I am blowing out the lamp for you." The lamp sputtered.

I will read Fred's new letter in the morning.

Dear Cousin Dawn,

The Nazi came back. At midnight, on top the cliffs, Marie and I watched him get out of the U-boat down below us in the cove. The boy, as Mrs. G. calls him, rows him to shore. I never see him bring bags with him, except a small pack over his shoulder, yet Marie informs me the locked room is now more full of gold than ever. We think the gold comes through Canada and is distributed to various hideouts. Marie said she got bold to ask him what he is doing here, and he replied, "I work for the Vaterland."

Marie laughed then and said her land is France—"la patrie,"

and hadn't he best mind his mouth? (Mrs. G. wasn't in the room.)

He said, "It is then a competition of countries in this very room on this island. When our Vaterland rules, you, Marie, will understand how good life will be."

"What will your Motherland do to make my life any better?" she asked him.

"I will build a castle for you on this island. Such a beautiful French face will attract a fine German officer to live with you," he replied.

Marie took his finished plate to the kitchen and told the cook to serve him dessert. That if she had to hear one more insanity from this man, she would hysterically scream, which would bring Mrs. G. downstairs. And the Nazi would love that.

Mrs. G.'s niece continues to ride a horse each day over the island, visiting every place and minding everyone's business. The young stranger has faded, and now the niece is in love with the Nazi officer himself. Her aunt is very jealous. The niece told Marie and the cook she got invited on board the U-boat, and her aunt is not to know this.

"What is in that boat?" Marie asked her.

"Guns and items to be stored in my aunt's house, and then there is more gold. I am to be very rich when Germany conquers America." The niece tossed her head. Marie said it was disgusting, and she leaves the niece alone now at night, serving her and disappearing back into the kitchen.

Marie is happy, however, despite the mounting pressure of the Nazi's boasts. Her brother, Jack, is here, and when I talk to him about Lizzie, his eyes get soft, and he blushes when I ask him if he wishes to visit her. I show him her photograph. I'm not in love with Lizzie, so I don't mind. I think I see a future match, and I am going to encourage Jack to visit you and Matt. Would you please take him to a dance and make sure Lizzie attends? Jack plays the fiddle, and I can assure you that Lizzie, once she hears him play, will have eyes for no one else.

I am not a family man. I would only make Lizzie unhappy. Her life would be a quiet torment with me, and she might always be worrying over my impulsiveness and irascibility. You think I wasn't part of dynamiting the Nazis' home. Well, it was mostly my idea. I have to be cautious until this Nazi mess gets cleared up. This other fellow recently came out here, and I'm staying clear of him. I tell Marie to do the same. Keep her mouth shut, talk only in French if she has to explode at him. Marie and I are such a pair, "peas in a pod," they say out here.

These Germans try to be gentlemen, dressing for dinner with gold tie clips and cuff links and dinner jackets and shoes shined each day by the Nazi boy who sits in the sun on a bench beside the house, looking east across the cove. I ask him—I hardly ever go into the Big House—if he likes taking care of the men, and he replies in broken English that there is nothing better to do in life than lean back on this bench, shine shoes, and observe the sea.

The way I see my life—I am looking for a chance to earn some money, then to find another job with no politics following me: where I can get far from talk of the war.

Fondest greetings to my family, and tell my pa a letter is on its way, regular mail. When I write you, I smuggle my letter off island with a lobsterman. It is a fact that Mrs. G. reads the island mail in the post office before it goes off on the mail boat. It would be death for me if any news of my stories of the island Nazis reached the mainland. The postmistress saw Mrs. G. reading my recent letter to Pa and Ma. Letters to them, of course, only contain trivial news, and I always praise Mrs. G. in them. As a result, she recently raised my wages.

Love,
Cousin Fred

P.S. Hope your paintings are going well.

They were. My second painting sold. It depicted infinity in the present. It is not a scene of hope, where time is unfound. This one showed heaven to be right before me. The mountains and sky are endless distances, with paths—which take time to walk. The beginning of the path is oil paint on the canvas. The rest of the journey commences. A skywalk then stretches into the stars.

You can paint numerous types of clouds. You can devise new cloud forms, yet there is a signpost for each direction of the sky. Clouds are the atmosphere that surrounds us. Goethe, Mam said, could remember a progression of clouds in a week. He learned to predict weather over a fortnight by remembering the past clouds. She said look to the evening

sky. I painted twilight before dusk descends. I also could tell weather
from these clouds.

Now news of the war made daily life incredibly discordant. Clouds
changed to mackerel patterns in the sky. And I was cross with this. War
jars you like crows squawking in mid air, chasing the bald eagle. Leave the
eagle alone! you want tell those crows. No one here wanted us to enter
into it, judging by the arguments on the store porch. I listened to this
squabble until my imagination took refuge beyond the river cove. I could
not sleep, but lay awake until daybreak.

The radio sputtered in rainstorms. Uncle and his family listened as
they ate supper. Matt gave up listening at his house, joining the farmers
who gathered after work to listen to the radio at the store. There was
better reception there, he said. Mr. B. kept the screen door unlocked until
dark. When war is close, everyone is on edge.

Uncle said some think the president is paying too much attention to
the international news, and if our own village can deal with Nazi spies,
smoking them out, then why does our country have to fight them abroad?
If the government would make it legal for towns and small villages to
oust the Nazis—shoot them out of the air— then why involve the entire
country at war for other countries? It makes no sense.

"The government will never do that—that is for sure," Aunt said.
"Never give us little people our own means to deal with evil."

"How do you know it is evil?" asked Jeremy, Fred's brother.

"It is true that we don't know that for sure," Uncle replied to him. It
was breakfast, which I still made for them.

Only after the war, we in this village learned about the Nazi
concentration camps.

"Well, why do we believe the government will get involved in the
European war, if they didn't believe us about our Nazis here? Sure
resisted helping us," I said. Matt was away, still haying at his grandfather's
farm next village over the hill. I thought how I'd be avoiding this talk if
I were at his house.

"Dawn is right in asking that. We always come back to that question.
Why would they fight the war abroad, when we were terrified right here
in our village, and they turned a blind eye?" Uncle said. "We just have to
keep to our guns and our own means of dealing with our problems." He
breathed deeply, letting out his breath. I was sure he thought about his
son, Fred, in that moment. A tear shone on his lashes. Maybe Uncle was
not so harsh; I frowned at my own judgment of him.

Looking back, we didn't know what being a Nazi meant nor the horrors that they inflicted. Here in the village, we smelled them like foxes, that nasty urine smell. Hunting in the night, they claimed their territories. What we puzzled about was the radio news reporting that Hitler daily was getting more powerful. I think we felt this meant he was focusing on Europe, so our village and the Nazis conquering Maine remained remote, never to happen. And of course we were right.

"Well, we have proof," Matt insisted, whenever I brought up the house bombing and how the village was so sure of Nazis living in it; could they be counter-spies? "Their guilt is obvious. Proof they were up to no good. The housekeeper for the Nazis took papers from their bedrooms before the house was blown sky high. There was detailed information on every villager who visited the store, and the meetings that the two Nazis went to in Lewiston. It was mostly in German. It took a while to find a translator. Fred said the papers got sent to the president, who, of course, completely ignored them. Uncle has the copies of the papers. Proof solid for the spring floods to sweep away a year's garbage."

℃ℜ ℜ℃

The path to the river was worn in irregular footprints. They say you can step in ruts and never see how to smooth them out. As I walked, I thought about the issue Matt constantly brought up. "If America goes to war, I want to enlist, rent out my farm. Ma can live with my grandfather."

"You know your ma and I will scream at once, pounding on her kitchen table, making the plates clatter: no, because the cows will die; your ma and I cannot keep them all milked."

We used frank language with him—die. More likely we'd sell them. Matt had brought this up before we married, and I was quiet about it, until now. He couldn't stop listening to the radio.

"If Germany declares war on America, as it might, I'll go."

No one really thought seriously that Germany would do this. We cast aside that thought. We had thousands of safe, ocean miles between us.

"You are joking, of course," I said one day as we swam, and I held him under water. He had to reply to me. I was not letting him go to a senseless war.

"They think they will conquer us by infiltrating our country. Look at the Nazis passing through our village. And the government is so stupid to ignore this. Why, I think the next one will be skinned and dumped in the river, which happened, remember, to the farmer."

Well, I shut up. I've mentioned this story before. It is never over being shocking to people, for it comes up still in many conversations. It always makes me shudder. But I wasn't to say stop referring to it. I'd speak constantly of the shock of my mother's death. Grief takes a long time to leave. So, I just listened now to anyone bringing old stories up.

After lunch, during this long midday break, when the entire village goes home to eat and rest, Matt and I swam and then went uphill to his farm, where his ma and I discussed the problem further with him.

"Think I should go?" Matt asked this so softly I didn't think I'd heard him right. He leaned back in the chair and let out a loud belch. Then Ma gripped her juice glass, and I covered my mouth almost in relief, not embarrassment. You see, I thought Matt was deciding to give in to his mother, look after her and the farm life, putting his thoughts of joining the war behind him.

I said, "Going to war, if you are a farmer, is like saying you're done with the land, feeding the animals and people. Done with the demands of the village, the twenty-four-hour vigilance over cattle, sheep, when they are ill or giving birth."

We sat in front of a window in his ma's kitchen; a slight breeze brushed through the screen. I could see the eagle across the valley. From here, a pretty view: the river winding and the mountain against the horizon. Blue haze shimmered over the distant ridges.

When you have to make decisions, you can lie under stars, Mam said. Stare into them. If sleep comes, you may have a prophetic dream, which points you on the path. I like to think that if there are other people out there, we are all together in this vast place, and my own life seems small. "I could spend my life just going for the ride," I once said to Mam. Pa thought it was a fine idea, like riding the Ferris wheel at the country fairs all your life. There is a wheel which turns that Ferris wheel, I thought. Who was turning the earth?

Matt and I watched how the stars were lights of cities, infinite homes, of which only the windows revealed life. Mam told me, "We float. Our soul leaves our body, blown upwards, joining our loved ones for a short time. Then we awake from sleep, forgetting our reunions. This is where we go."

"Is this where we will go permanently when we die?"

"I believe it is. We rise up like a bee on a spring morning. We land on a blossom. Then we blow like wind on bushes. We have invisible arms to hold on and keep on with people we love on earth."

I remember asking her if a wind was going to take her. She said, "When I am ready." I looked at the stars; they quivered.

After watching the stars, we sat at the table in silence, with Matt's ma staring to the mountains into Canada. Silence is unnerving when so much is unknown.

"Why would America enter the war?" his ma asked for the hundredth time. She sipped yarrow tea at night. Said it kept her liver from disturbing her sleep. Her mug clattered as she placed it on the table. She had cut her hair. She wore dungarees. I wondered what my own mother would have looked like in these modern times.

As I ate a bowl of cornflakes, I thought about war and how it brought such sadness back to me, because I wasn't sure about Matt. He appeared calm, fixed on something, like a deer pausing at the forest edge.

Takes time to let someone pass. You come to the edge of a place where you cannot find them. Then you slip off the edge into the shadow lands, and you find the person; you bring them into light; your memory of them is light for them. I know this to be so. Mam is with me even now, and it is my turn soon to go. To say I was over Mam's passing by any age, it wouldn't be true. Like telling this story now—I don't know if I'll stop in the middle of it, or someplace I will call the end. Maybe at my own baby's passing, or before it. There is only so much you can tell others.

If Fred hadn't left, had the idea of bombing a house, got the village to do it for him, then fled; if he'd just stayed on, I'd never have married early, been forever in love with my cousin, and never looked at anyone else. Just let him marry Lizzie, and keep my fondness for my cousin as a brother I never had. The Nazis should never have come to our village.

Fear whips its own horse, and none of us did that. Fear comes when you think things are destroyed. Fear can tweak a valley from the way it was used to being. So I made sure I kept settled. Fear leaves then. As we've seen. That's how a country gets strong again after war. Some who die because of fear; others who fear because they live on. Living on: Mam said you pass on the trade of hard work.

Each night I lay awake. I knew that Fred was in danger, with knowledge of island gold more dangerous than my river gold hidden for centuries in dark caves. You know, not hidden by humans, only the earth itself. I said I wasn't taking more of those nuggets, but I did, putting them to my studio drawer under the paints. Fred might need them.

Mam said sleep is sometimes the hardest job; she'd lie awake after a difficult day of work. I went over ways of getting my cousin off the island. Then I'd lie awake trying to imagine Mam back, and then I'd drift on adventures where I climbed cliffs, rafted rivers, and walked landscapes

I had never seen in actual life, just to find her. These were dreams of anguish, and yearning.

Then, when I became close friends with Matt, he helped me feel I had a place on earth; I found my mother's home fixed up: my painting began, as if she had returned. By autumn, I was launching a career in nursing. It was carrying on Mam's work.

Next day a letter arrived.

Dear Cousin Dawn,

Nights are getting cold. Guess what? Another stranger is on the island. He was on the path to the Big House as I passed him. I asked him what he carried. He said a painting. He was going to see a friend.

I left him because I was walking fast to Old Grumble's at the end of day. I was tired and didn't want to talk. I noticed the stranger's accent was similar to the Nazi officer's.

Now I am worried, Dawn. Two strangers arriving very recently. Did I tell you the first one came through our village? He saw you with your herbs, only you refused to speak with him. Thank you. I refused to answer his question: did I know you? I carry Old Grumble's pistol with me now. I am not going to end up thrown into the ocean: the stranger asked me if I'd heard about a house being blown up in our village, and I told him no. I lie, but I have to save my soul.

Old Grumble looked intently at me this morning. It is turning out he is smarter than I thought. He said carry the pistol all the time. "Go to work, talk to no strangers, stay away from Mrs. G. and her guests, even the niece." Never speak to Marie in sight of the Big House. Bring Marie to this cabin if we need to talk, and tell her that she is in danger.

I am not used to this danger, Dawn. I almost long now for my father's cows and the backbreaking farm work. This is not my idea of life anymore, out here on the island.

Today I mentioned to Jack, Marie's brother, I might be deciding to leave. He said he's turning a blind eye to the affairs at the Big House, except to be pleasant to Mrs. G.—that I'd best do the same, unless I had a plan of how to leave the island and what I'd do back on the mainland.

He's right. If I come home, Liz will be all over me, and I'll feel obliged to settle down. I am going to roam some more. I like Marie. She's fun. We see life the same way. She is lonely out here.

Jack is organizing a dance. He says to talk to everyone but the Nazis and to stay calm. A frolicsome attitude takes away suspicion. He thinks it would be good for the island to have some fun after the drowning of the boy and the gossip about the Germans.

Jack, Marie, and I watch the new stranger being rowed out to the U-boat. We watch this boat get fueled up from the island tank. The U-boat goes off on journeys then returns. The same officer gets out to see Mrs. G. and stay with her. The strangers live in the U-boat now.

Today I visited the professor on my way home from work. He let me listen to his radio. It sure crackles out here. I feel sorry for the countries fighting each other. Why can't people live quietly, tend their farms or professions and not have to fight? Politicians are evil, Dawn. If politicians had volunteer jobs and no one paid them for being in office, they'd get their jobs done quickly. They'd go home to other jobs. I'm not for entering the war. No one wants our country in another world war, do they?

The professor told me that he went over various options, but he didn't have clarity about what I should do with my future. I think once I get an idea about what I want to do in my life, something will let me leave the island. If you have any ideas for me, I've never asked you this: please let me know. I'll come back to the mainland, if I can think of what to do.

Give my regards to Matt and his ma. Do not mention me to Lizzie. Jack has started to write her. Even from a distance, he is certain he loves her.

Your cousin,
Fred

Next letter, a month later, November, 1941:

Cousin Dawn,

The Big House is lit up; the cook has an assistant who helps in the kitchen. There are three to four Nazis dining there, and Marie is constantly upset with them. She speaks to them in French because not only she is following advice to stay out of danger, but she is also very annoyed with them. They speak in their language almost all the time. I think Mrs. G. seems to understand them quite well. One of the Germans answered Marie back in French, saying he didn't know France was hoping to take over Maine, and he winked at her. He said, "Maine will be the first state Germany conquers, so be careful, our little French darling." Marie did laugh when he said that. But she retorted she'd fire the first shot at them. He looked startled and backed away because she reached into her apron pocket. She was sure he knew she carried a gun.

The dance went well. With enemies swinging together, I wondered why I am being so anxious, for everything will be just fine. Why do I distrust anybody? How ridiculous I have become. So I am relaxing and reckoning that Mrs. G. has international money interests, not actually politics. She wants to be extremely rich. She is focused only on herself, and I will be safe somehow. I am leaving worries behind tonight. I don't think she will harm me.

Your cousin,
Fred

I had no time to dwell on Fred's life. I was working hard, up at dawn to milk his cows and preparing Auntie's breakfast and lunch, the main meal, for her family. Then I was free to race to my home, tend the herbs, get them harvested. I had a room full of them drying on trays. I had to start work soon with the midwife, as soon as a baby came due. Then, in spare time, I painted and was a wife to my husband at night, when we sat at supper with his ma, and we slept in his deep bed; it was a century old.

I almost put Fred's letters in the woodstove. So what if he was in danger. It was his fault. However, I took them back to the shoebox. More arrived weekly.

Dear Dawn,

You told me to write about my thoughts of Matt wanting to fight abroad. Will he be heading first to England? Tell him to wait. He should not leave. If he leaves his farm, it will be lost. Even renting it out can bring it to ruin. He is the only one to carry it on. The English can fight their own war. Old Grumble says if Germany captures England, as it is looking that it will, it'll do the

English some good. I know no British, so I can't understand what he means.

He pointed to a photograph of a young girl on his mantel. She was British, he explained. "I fell in love with her. I was in World War I. I visited her parents, and they told her she could not marry me. I was from a Maine island in America with no money. She cried, and I nearly wept too, but I bit my lip and left her." He took the photo and held it before him.

She's no doubt an old woman, bless her, with grandchildren. I cannot forget her, but I cursed her parents when I left her. I never looked back. Damn Brits."

I was sad on hearing that story. It seems this Maine island has people with pasts unimaginable, unless they share their stories in some moment. Perhaps that is like that anywhere. Old Grumble drew in his breath, tapped his pipe on the table by his chair, reminding me of hollow knocks on doors, the kind you have to run from, not answer. He exhaled the sweet-smelling tobacco smoke around the crackling fire. I lay back on my pillow and watched the flames. They lit up the rafters above me.

Tell Matt he'd be a fool to leave you, my dear.

Love,
Cousin Fred

Finished the third large painting—a still life of a flower and vase. Not an action painting, it is quiet, the subtle colors capture detail in symbolic form. The vase is a vessel into which you put your life. I took Mam's favorite vase, set it on her kitchen table, then found chrysanthemums by the garden shed, exposed to the southern sky.

Years later, I reflected on this painting and what I left out of it: the small details of both Mam and Matt. How, as I painted, he sat and watched me, while I thought about Mam. Mam stood beside me. She touched my hand as the colors appeared on my paper; Matt with his gaze on me clasped my eyes. Sometimes he sat with me half a day, not looking at me but reading, leaning back in my pa's old chair. That day I paid no attention to him; I got so absorbed in the colors that when I looked up to see him—he was gone. I shrugged and let him go. His presence seemed still there, that gaze on me with his eyes. For me, that was what mattered.

I remember how farmwork slowed to rest, except for cows to milk. Nights cooled as harvesting wound down; dances resumed. Shoes polished to brilliant shining, matches lit cigarettes, and courtship began. Who would dance with Lizzie? I wondered about her pining for Fred. Would it continue? I reflected on Matt and his love and my caution of love.

"Love can grow," Mrs. B. kept telling me. "Let it ripen and wait for it."

I listened to her, thinking that for Matt and me it was a good thing to be in basic routines. Working for Aunt, growing plants, painting. They carry you on, when you are least thinking about a day.

"Take it each day at a time," Mrs. B. said.

Sometimes one person continues to love and can never make the partner love them back in the same way. That was my fear for Matt. I might not love him as much as he wished me to. One of the village stories, which scared me about the betrayal of true love, was this one: The school music teacher got married one spring, and then in the autumn, when we returned to classes, it was over. She loved him terribly. We wondered, as kids will do, was she good enough for him? They said his eyes shifted about in church, as if his mind couldn't settle down. People said he was excessively busy. No time for love. He left her one day and never came back to his home. Then, the next year, he married one of his students, but that ended unhappily. The student died six months later of tuberculosis. Our village that year was fearful that others would come down with it. No one did. And no one felt sorry for him. His first wife moved away. What did she ever see in him anyway? people asked. Mrs. B. said that love is just like that. You never can tell.

Matt and I might have a chance—being good friends when we married. I hold this true that if sun shines on a plant it will rise. The day of my beginning my fourth painting, when he watched me attentively, perhaps not daring to speak, instead of only looking at my colors on paper, I took a break and went to sit in his lap. It felt like sun shining there.

He sat barely moving, letting the day flow on. I got up to make tea, but we drank Pa's elderberry wine instead. Then we walked into the night fog, crossing the iron bridge to the other side of the river. We went up the hill to his house, where his ma had left a gas lamp glaring, she having gone to bed so early at dusk, because, according to habit, she always got up at 4 a.m. I thought, when I get that old, I will love that hour, too. Eternity dips low in stillness. I felt a blink from Mam then.

With nights getting chilly, when we got home we put wood on the fire, blew out the lamp, fell into bed. This was the part I loved the most: curling into each other, as if we protected our bodies while our minds slept.

But I lay awake. How could Matt wish to leave this happiness for war? He tells me people in London have to suffer bombings from the Germans. Yet don't we deserve the peace we have been born to, which our parents worked hard to create? Lead a simple life, Mam had said.

"It doesn't seem right, when I have happiness, that other people are fighting and dying." Matt had said that night. "Can you imagine what England will be like when Germany takes over?" He told me more deeply why he wished to help this country fight off Germany. He was connected to England because his father came from London to settle in America. He wanted land and to grow gardens, have cows. He had saved enough to buy one hundred acres on top of this hill. He called it Hill Farm.

That night wind rattled the shutters. As I lay listening, I heard all the fears of the village like conversations going through me, what actually would happen to us if Germany also took over our country. I supposed the English people felt the same fears, even more intensely. I felt I was wrong to keep Matt from helping his family's homeland. I buried my face in the long pillow we shared. Matt bent to kiss me one more time.

I endeavored to keep news out of our bedroom. Matt kept a small Bakelite radio, the latest rage, plugged in the kitchen by the door. He came in from work, switched it on before he even sat down. We depended on hearing the war's advance in Europe. Some of the news assured us America was keeping out of it, as it was far across the Atlantic, free from danger. I was sure if they knew German U-boats were fueling up on a Maine island, where Fred lived, they would not say we were safe. "They know," Mr. B. would insist. "Just—they don't care."

I faced the ceiling after Matt fell asleep. I pictured the people in the Big House on the island. I saw them dancing to that record player. Sometimes I read Fred's letters absorbing each detail of what he said. I pictured what it was like to be out on an island, dancing, eating, laughing, as if mindlessness were the best attitude to adopt to face the impeding war. I couldn't imagine that Fred only looked in the windows. Yet he assured me he stayed clear of his employer's parties.

And I wanted my painting back. The painting the stranger had carried was mine. The one that had been bought outside Mr. B.'s store. Fred wrote me not to sell anymore paintings there, so I will find a gallery in Portland to display them, where only regular tourists attend. He said the Nazi had a daughter who resembled me but who was ill, so the father is bringing this painting to her.

Of course, I cannot want my painting back. He said that the girl loves to paint. He will keep it on her wall. Even as an old man, he will remember Maine because of my painting. I liked that part. I wished I had spoken more to this man. Did the Nazi suspect I knew Fred? No, Matt was sure he didn't, as long as Fred kept very quiet on the island. If they discover he instigated the bombing of the village house, they will kill him.

I didn't think I should call all Germans Nazis. I rested uneasily over this. Mam had read German poets to me. Her favorite German poem was by Goethe, and I had learned it in German. *"Über allen Gipfeln / Ist Ruh . . ."* Mam had said it quieted her at night to read this because it was like our village. If someone in Europe could feel the same way that we did about peace, then wasn't this a means of finding a way to end wars and understand each other, through literature? Mam posed questions to me that I instinctively grasped. "Guess so, Mam."

She said that even greater than literature was philosophy, ideas, and that this study transcended all things. Ideas of the universe never die.

Most travelers crossed the Canadian border, just north of our village, on a small road, with few people interested in who comes and goes. Fred had said the man with my painting was best friends with the German commander of the U-boat, where he now slept each night. Fred assumed he helped keep things undercover. Fred heard rumors that another U-boat was coming into harbor soon. The cook had overheard the dinner-table conversation. The cook, terrified, told Marie to warn Fred. I guess Marie was crying because she didn't want anymore Germans in more U-boats and more work, more beds to make. The cook and maid were paid well, Fred said. When she gets off the island, Marie will use the money to go to business school on the mainland.

CR   CR

December 7 came. And I tell you, war makes madness. The village gathered at the store to talk about Pearl Harbor. Men shouted. Anger lines creased their usually passive faces. They carried pitchforks, I don't know why. I stood to the side of the crowd, holding Matt's dog on a rope. I needed animal company, and I stroked her fur. This anger was more explosive than the exhilaration over the bombing of the Nazis' house in our village. This emotion was as a river flood, sweeping people's homes, lives downstream, and everything was about to change. I trembled, because Matt was part of that crowd.

Then Mr. B. rattled a large tin can filled with pennies. "Take out your cigarettes, pipes, and calm down," he bellowed. "I want silence, right now, in front of my store. This moment is important, so let me speak."

The mood of the people at the store was quiet, in fact, deathly still. I held onto the dog very tightly. Already the men had lit up, with faces grim set. For moments, all you could see was smoke above everyone. Just a few women smoked. Mrs. B. and I did. She was sitting on her chair, as usual, binoculars around her neck, head high, elegantly blowing a large ring, from a long cigarette. Normally I would laugh, because so tiny, hunched over, she didn't look as if she held a government job.

"You can go home to your own radios and listen to the president. But let's have it clear right here. I'll turn up the radio, and you can hear it first as a community. We stick together in this. Japan declared war on us, and Germany has done so as well. We have, as of today, Sunday, December 7, entered into the war."

He continued, "You all know what that means. Any German sneaking over the border stepping into my store from now on is an enemy. Period. I am done with being nice to strangers. Let me repeat this: we are at war. If the government doesn't care about our village dealing with these outsiders, then we will take our own action again, is that clear?"

There was a roar greater than the water in April bursting over the dam. Amid the tobacco smoke, I could see a passion born. Villagers' eyes became fiery red. I felt nauseous, putting out my own cigarette and clutching the dog. We have become barbarians here, I thought, and someone shot off a gun over our heads.

I searched for Matt. I found him sitting on a stone fence to the side of the store. He was alone, smoking. He didn't see me. The dog nuzzled his fingers, yelped as smoke went in its eyes. Drew back, looked askance. Matt reached out to touch him, but he was cold to me. His thoughts had no way to connect with mine.

People drifted apart or in clusters in this village gathering. Snow started to fall like goose feathers spilling from pillows. Grannies still shook out these feather pillows from village windows each morning.

The snow got heavy. Still the crowd stayed at the village store, wanting more war news. Women started getting the men home by screaming at them. I knew a radio sat beside each home's woodstove, but no matter the season, the men listened to the one in the store. In addition, there was some sense in smoking and discussing war together.

Next morning the crowd was back at the store. Some men carried guns. Everyone looked for strangers in the village now. Any hiding in barns? In attics? No German would come out alive from our village.

Before I left my aunt's house, I made butter from thick cream. As I hung up my apron, I thought how nothing was right now. I wanted Mam to hear me.

Mr. B. put up a sign, gathered his hammer and nails, and went back into the store. Men inched closer to see. Women and children held back. Monday work was cancelled, the factory doors shut. People read signs on every door. Someone in the night had posted signs for enlisting in the war. Some people were already throwing stones at them.

Mr. B. shook his tin can again. I could use some of those pennies, I was thinking.

The hush rolled over the ground like a January thaw. "No violence here. No throwing stones. Government may not have helped us with our Germans, but that's no reason to forsake our country in this dire time. What Mrs. B. and others did all summer, watching airplanes—was government work. So, they aren't going to leave us be now. We'll keep working for them. I know none of you like how we had to deal with our own situation, and it was apathy towards us in the North. Might as well join Canada, I know some of you say."

He stopped for a second. "I am asking every one to put away your guns. No man will be shot at here. If there are Germans in this crowd, they can walk away. No one will shoot them, is that understood?" Men looked away and slightly shifted their pistols and rifles. The ones who didn't bear firearms rolled cigarettes and exhaled.

Mr. B. continued, "Who wants to be conquered by another country? None of us. We have to fight them first overseas and keep eyes on the ones here, which we already do—right? So, we're ahead of the government. Mrs. B. here will tell you that. She's been informing Washington, DC all along of air traffic. And anyone looking like a Nazi."

Mrs. B. sat on the store porch in her chair and blew out her smoke. After every sentence, her husband paused to look at her, and she nodded.

"All men, whether you've got a farm or none, have to report for the draft. You have to sign up now to register. The government will decide if they leave you on your farm or not. Here's the paper; here's the pens. The draft board is here at this store. Come along, and no running off. We're going to win this war!" he shouted with Mrs. B. shaking her fist at the sky.

The crowd roared again. "Mam," I whispered as I stood there, "the colors are turning brown, dark blood on my paper; my paints are swirling of their own mind; my hand is numb, and I can't find a way to hold my brush."

I turned and ran up the hill with the dog behind me. Matt wasn't here in this Monday crowd. He had to finish milking. I had to tell him something first, before he went to sign that paper. He had to be excused from war, O please! I lifted my eyes. Snow was viciously blowing. I saw the steep trail off the mountainside, and the weather was locked into a pattern. I was catching my breath, feeling faint.

The woodstove churned; green logs hissed. The drier wood waited inside the shed for January. I sat down to rest. Matt rushed into the room, looked straight ahead. "Matt," I quietly called. He turned, not seeing me, not believing I was there.

I wanted to keep the secret. I was saving it to tell him in my studio, in my own home where I felt comfortable, memory fortifying me to go on. Here, I was still a stranger in Matt's territory. Not able to put myself in it. I had to learn the ways of his house from his ma.

"Something to tell you." I whispered, and he spun around.

"Shh," he said, "my head hurts. Have to talk later." He went outside; I didn't try to stop him. The door slammed; the handle wobbled. I brought another log to the stove, put it in and bent over to think.

Let things be, Mam would say.

He didn't come home that night. I stayed at his home during the next day. Cleaned the house, made bread, talked to his ma. Small conversations we had, because we left the radio alone. What is war to us? I thought. I smelled bread baking. The wooden floor shone after the waxing I'd given it. We couldn't leave; our anger was personal. I could paint my anger, see how my fingers took the brush. Explore what colors came out of fear. But I wasn't leaving the village on account of war.

That next night Matt came home; he slept curled on the edge of the bed. I cried softly, almost through the night, face smothered against the goose down. Stiff dreams churned butter with my wooden paddles. We did not lie entwined. Our hands couldn't enter sleep as on a path together.

I slept for a while and awakened. I trod past the creaky boards, skipping three. Fed the cats, stoked the fire, rushed to the sink to vomit. I opened the door to let the cats out, and that's when I heard Mam calling me. I stepped barefoot on the snow. Mam wasn't there. I went back in, put on coat, boots, hat, took the lantern from the wall hook. Walked down the hill, across the bridge, along the lane to my own house.

Mam opened the door there for me. I ran into her arms. Pa came to carry his little girl to his rocking chair. "Mile of snow, beating wind, wet mass of hair to dry," he said. Mam looked on. Rock, creak, lift off the ground, forward speed, back to sleep, little one, little one.

Fighting tears, this battle got me wounded before it began. Fields were inching deeper with the snow. Venus buried behind the river hill.

When I woke, I saw that firewood was stacked beside the door. Automatically I got up to put more wood on the fire, figures of Mam and Pa gone, my mind creating reality to lure me to unconscious mind, as a death sleep dissolves rocks, stones.

I jumped with the thought of red coals gone black. "Never let the stove go out in the Northland," Pa told me before he left for the west coast. My eyes opened fully then. Fire roared. Who stacked the wood, made the kitchen warm? I carried the logs to the old Ashley and sat by it, turning to the counter, catching a feeling of something out of place. My paints stored in the cupboard, brushes in a jar, easel by the window.

A single piece of paper with a pencil laid on it. I fingered the note's edge, pulling it to me. It was from Matt and said,

Dear Dawn,

If you read this, having come here to paint tonight, know I love you and thank you for becoming my wife. I am glad you are independent because that is the right kind of a person. Then I think you will understand I have that desire do something that is rising as a passion in me. I need to go now to serve the country in this war. I will start in England, then, hopefully, move on wherever I am needed. I cannot let England be taken over, and neither can I bear to see this country flounder. Maybe I should stay on the farm, but your uncle is taking my cows, and Ma is going to be fine alone. She will have always have that home.

I trust you will live at your own home, and know my thoughts are with you—in the paintings you will do, and your new job helping the midwife in winter. I trust you will follow your mother in nursing, but not forget your painting. I loved watching you. It is peaceful, calming; you are so focused with your painting. Your true place is here. Don't forget it is your passion, for if it gets gruesome, it is no longer what you love. Balance your life. If at some point in your life the love has gone, then step back, look out the window in your mother's kitchen, and figure what is not right. My ma tells me it's a matter of putting the right things in their place.

When you read this, I'll be gone. I am on my way to Boston; we ship out mid-week for basic training. In a few years, I'll return home to you, Dawn. I know you'll keep things going for yourself, even if your heart is full when you read this. I hope I didn't claim you too young in your life. I worried about this, seeing your beauty growing and your potential at painting blooming. You could go anywhere, step into a ball gown, and glide with the dance music. When I think like this, I tell myself, Dawn is more real than my worry. That other Dawn is my imagination, and even though she may have a future beyond my picturing of her, she has her home, her work. Perhaps I helped in a small way. I lit the fire for you this early morning, figuring I'd slip away before you could stop me.

> Your loving husband,
> Matt

I clutched my stomach, rushed to the sink. I found crackers to eat and sipped water. My unfinished painting faced me; I took a paintbrush, dipped it into paint, willed my hand to touch the paper. I swirled the brush into water, put it into more paint and then again on the paper. I could never look backwards. Sand lay deeply in the river cove, and come spring I could hunt gold.

Mam and Pa were behind me, seeing me paint, observing that inside of my belly a baby had begun, and I wouldn't tell Matt now, nor his ma, not even Fred. My work and paintings and this baby were one creation.

I worked for hours. Then I made tea, ate more crackers, washed out the paintbrushes, prepared to meet the midwife for the start of my job, which would soon give me the earnings to maintain my home, myself and my paintings. If not, there is the gold—this thought comforted me.

ങ ര

Light came on the hills and with it more snow falling. I put wood in the stove and took Mam's old comforter, wrapped it around me, and fell asleep on the chair until afternoon. I thought about Matt, how he had lain stiff beside me in bed. My fears made me sure it was the last time I'd ever sleep by his side.

A letter from Fred. I wanted to burn it. I needed Matt's words instead. Don't question the receiving, Mam would have said. Take what comes. I opened it with a kitchen knife.

Dear Cousin Dawn,

Father wrote me that Matt left for Europe. I had no idea of this. I guess he was more reckless than anyone knew, needing a break from the farm too. So I'm not the only one wishing to get away from tradition and strike out on adventure. Here I was envying you both settling down, and now I am so sorry for you.

Are you managing? Is my old Dawn there inside of you? The philosophical, determined Dawn? She will return. Don't you worry about that.

Jack is leaving the island and enlisting. He will first stop by the village to meet Lizzie. They've been courting by letter. He wants to see her "in the flesh," he says. When he says it like this, he rubs his hands together and gets such a red face.

He's going to visit her for a couple weeks before he ships out to his war training. That is, if they get along as well as they do in their letters. I tell him: You're going to have to come back home to her after war's over, prove you're the kind of fellow she's happy about being with all her life. Jack likes when I say this, because he says it suits him well. He wants a girl with him day and night, too, but this war is interfering with them now, oh for sure.

I am going to try to leave in the next few weeks. Mrs. G. says it's impossible, because she needs my help though the winter. The professor says she is forbidding me to leave. She is fearful that I have seen something. He says I am in tough, dangerous water.

A U-boat came in last night. Marie and I watched it slowly surface. The officer getting off it greeted Mrs. G.'s German officer, and they went up to the Big House. Marie said they dined with plenty of wine, and the radio blasted the war news.

She said the room in the house is still filling up with ornaments of gold, gold picture frames with pictures taken from them. The U-boats fuel up, then, after a few days, leave. She said the officers speak in German, so she can't understand what is happening.

Marie told Mrs. G., with our country getting into the war, this island now has the enemy on it. Marie has some guts to say this. Mrs. G. hissed at her. She told Marie these officers are her friends. Friendship goes beyond war. Marie felt saucy to go on talking. She said that these are only recent friends. Mrs. G. replied she was a silly goose. That she has known one of the officers for a very long time, long ago, in a time when she didn't live on the island.

Mrs. G. looked hard at Marie and told her be careful what she speaks about.

I will write you more soon again. Give us a kind thought, knowing I think of you constantly.

Your cousin,
Fred

During this time, the snow came and stayed. White transformed the village into tiny lanes, snow piled high. I passed through the lanes at night, on my way home from working with the midwife. I looked into people's houses, which were glowing with gas lamps. I think many tears fell behind those windows, but mine froze outside on my eyelashes. A change happened between Mam and me. It disturbed me: Mam looked at me from behind these people's windows, not directly out of her own window. She didn't stand beside me in the cold.

In one home, there was a poster print of a family at a table and a Thanksgiving meal set before them. It was the holiday season. Even in wartime, I marveled there was abundance inside these homes. No curtains were drawn. I could stay a very long time to observe what decorations were being placed inside.

I decided I would paint these things, take these soft images of families in their homes and draw them. They'd be in my heart, even if I couldn't have them in real life. "Dawn," I'd say, "it's not possible with Mam gone, Pa traveling, and Matt to war." I talked out loud to myself. "Be sensible; return to your house and sleep warmly by the woodstove."

Cousin Dawn,

Said I'd write you again soon. We had to get Marie off the island since my last letter. Mrs. G. locked her in a third-floor room in the Big House. Mrs. G. wanted to leave on the U-boat with her Nazi. She told Marie to tell no one what she saw. Marie had asked Mrs. G. if she were a double spy, letting our government know about the Germans on the island, while giving them secrets from America and, actually, fuel. You are aiding the enemy, she told her employer.

I guess that was going too far. That's when she was locked up. Marie was sure she'd be killed there. Marie escaped from the house, tied sheets together and let herself out her window, ran to me at Old Grumble's cabin, and I ran with her to a lobster boat, got her off with nothing but herself, the lobsterman and his pots. She left her scant belongings behind, her uniform, a few nice clothes, but she took her saved money in her pocket. At least she had her money.

I don't worry about her as I write you this. The lobsterman got her to safety. He made sure she is back with her family on the coast. Yet, she fears to stay with them, aware that Mrs. G. might have Germans hunt her down there. I think she will find a place to hide. She daren't come to our village, with the Nazis having been there already searching you out as to what you knew.

Mrs. G., before she left, went on horseback all over the island looking for her maid. No one confessed to seeing her. I was honest with her. I said most likely Marie found someone to take her off island, the sensible thing to do. She stared at us, Old Grumble as if the devil could take us, but we didn't waver in what we said. She knew we couldn't carry her maid away.

Said she'd find who did it, and they'd lose their job. Ha! I grinned with Old Grumble after she left the cabin. No one is going to tell Mrs. G. They're all done with her, just about, even if she's their landlady. She's likely to end up floating in the ocean.

One thing I didn't tell you, Dawn. I am engaged to Marie. I pray you keep this news quiet. I plan to join her soon and get a war job in a factory in Massachusetts, making munitions on the coast. My eyesight won't let me join the Army, Jack said.

Your loving cousin,
Fred

I didn't hear any news of Matt. He disappeared out of my life. Nor did I hear from Fred for three weeks. I was very worried about them both. Jack arrived in our village, and I talked to him. He was staying with Lizzie. I went to a barn dance, where he was fiddling and she was dancing, and he watched her, winking at her as if she were the grandest lady. After the second week of Jack's being here, Lizzie whispered to me in Mr. B.'s store, "We are engaged. We are going to marry before Jack goes to war. I have one day to find a dress." I lent her mine.

☙ ☙

"We're war sisters now," Lizzie said to me and put her arm around me. I cried with no understanding of this bond of emotion with someone I used to despise and had lately grown to like because Fred didn't like her anymore. I didn't like my feelings as I sat next to Lizzie. Mr. B. had sat us down to hot cocoa before the woodstove. "You're my first customers this morning, the lovely glazed-eyed ladies. You both must make me a promise. You will come here each morning and chat with me. Keep me up on news of your sweethearts."

News wasn't yet out about Jack and Lizzie's secret, fast marriage in the minister's home.

Mr. B. patted our shoulders, for we still had arms about each other. Had us dry our boots before we left.

Mrs. B. came down the stairs in the store, with her day's knitting and binoculars stuffed in a basket. She prepared to sit behind the counter to wait on more people coming for groceries, newspapers, coffee and hot rolls. "I expect my job is soon over, watching for spy planes," she said.

Her husband said, "No, Mrs. B., they'll keep you hired. As long as the war is on, they'll need you looking for planes."

Mrs. B. looked pleased, took out her knitting. Her husband turned on the radio, then went outside to shovel snow from the porch steps.

"You look pale, Dawn," Mrs. B. said.

"I'm worrying about things too much, Ma'am," I told her. I didn't want anybody knowing about the baby, as I said. I didn't want Matt having to come home on account of me. I didn't wish him to give up his dream of fighting. He wanted to be gone. I was fine alone.

Mrs. B. looked sharply at me. Color came to my cheeks; I felt the heat prickle them. Then I took hold of Lizzie's hand and said aloud, so Mrs. B. heard, "Lizzie, we both have a lot to get used to. Seems like war rips a part of our guts out, doesn't it."

Mrs. B. then saw Lizzie's small band of gold on her ring finger, gasped, almost spilled her hot cocoa, and I knew my pale face was nothing compared to the sparkle of a marriage ring.

Dear Cousin Dawn,

I escaped from the island. Nazis poured in for one day, fueled up three U-boats, then left. The cook told me the room of gold was emptied. Marie had let her see the room, and I realized then we weren't the only ones to know and in danger. Cook said the gold was temporarily stored in the caves of the island, of course not all of it; there was too much. Mrs. G. boarded up the house, and she and her niece disappeared. Cook said they were both in love with the same Nazi officer, but realistically the niece will probably marry his son, who came for the father. Cook saw the smile light up in their eyes. The niece was something with the younger man with blue eyes, blond hair, and tall.

The island, Cook wrote me, is quiet. She doesn't cook at the Big House anymore, but works in the village café. She is sure Mrs. G. will return, open up the house in summer for guests, as she always has done. So Cook is content baking for the lobstermen.

I am with Marie, living in sin, in a small town where I got that job making munitions for the war. They say it is more dangerous than going to war. I have seen two men killed in ten days because machinery fell on them, swinging across the shop, unhooked.

By the time you read this, we will be married. Seems like war hurries some things up. I am happy with this girl. She is fun, and most of all loves life enough to trust it with me.

After the war is over, I am coming home with her. Mr. B. wrote me recently. He needs to turn the store over to a young man. I wrote him back and told him, "I am your man. I will work with you and slowly buy it from you."

You are my most darling cousin. You can tell my ma I will be writing her. Nothing is like it was, but everything is moving on. Isn't that something your mam would say?

Your cousin,
Fred

Epilogue.

After three years, Fred returned to our village and took over running the store. He married Marie. He didn't wish to farm. Said he could never love the work. He liked running a business. Mr. B and his wife retired above the store, happy to have him take over. They helped him until they could no longer walk up the rickety stairs.

The barn dances kept going, moving into the Grange Hall in winter. The same country-style music continued here. Fiddlers and bands jammed and kept the dance traditions. Jack came back from the war to Lizzie, and they had a child, a son.

Matt never came home. He died in Europe, close to the end of the war. I knew this would happen. I had prepared for this.

You see, Mam said to never look back if you feel a ghost is following you. Push on. I looked back on a day I knew he was dying and saw his spirit cross our river. If I hadn't seen that, he'd have lived; I know this. He needed to follow me until his strength returned; then I could look back and see him. It is a fact which I can say for all my life—it was my fault I lost him. Mam said to let this thought rush down the spring currents, but you know, you can't easily do that.

My work steadied me. Painting was my passion; nursing was my job. It was these two professions that saved me. I clung to work to forget grief. The baby that was ours, Matt's and mine, ah, this baby died of diphtheria in his second year. I lit a candle for him. I went to the river to tell Matt that the baby would be with him now, not me.

I put myself totally into my painting and my patients. My paintings sold in galleries. They fetched large sums. People wanted to see my eternal river valley.

I had to travel out of my valley, yet I always came home.

Fred and Marie had a wonderful life, as did Lizzie and Jack; the four were the best of friends. I went in and out of their lives. That is, I minded my own business and paid them visits when invited.

Pa came back to our village. Enough said. I cared for him and got him back to caring for animals, his work. It was tough love for me. I was still angry with him for leaving.

"Fred and the island Nazi" story got told in village circles, but no one knew where the gold went, nor where that Nazi captain ended up. Some said it had to be Argentina. Or, did Mrs. G. bury the gold on the island? After the war was over, Mrs. G. suddenly reappeared. She returned with her own airplane and took up flying around all the islands. No one knew why. No one knew how she got the money to buy her own plane. Thus, rumors spread about her.

Then, after the war, and this is God's truth, one of our village Nazis came back to tell us he was sorry for upsetting our village. He understood why we dynamited their house. He said that indeed they had been working for the Germans.

Our village has been privy to strangers. In September 2001, two strangers stopped at a store. In the autumn we have a few tourists viewing the colors of trees. The store owner, a friend of mine, saw their faces on the news; they had taken the plane from Portland to Boston and crashed it into the World Trade Center.

A season settles back into itself inland, even now. Storms churn, strangers pass; terror within this ill wind blows now and then. The village, the land, returns to its normalcy; I guess you'd say at the end of a year, you see reality as it is.

Mam comes to my bed wearing a white dress. The look in her eyes says, "Changes come, Dawn. You are old enough to accept this." She smiles. She said this to me as a child, when a pet had died. Her eyes look into mine. I am young, and she is the age when she left me.

I remember how Mam believed that everything here on earth has an association with something in Heaven. If form fills earthly space, then light illumines form. And this light comes from an immeasurable distance.

"When you leave, Dawn, you will pass out into this vastness. But it is filled with a substance of another material made with light, and sun. It will be your new body. Arms will hold you once more. Out there in the cold stars, I, your mam, will be there.

I look into a distance. I rise from my bed, and nurse gently puts me back on the bed. They are curious whom I see.

"Mam," I breathe. I try to forget earth so I can go. Yet, I want to remember one time more, sitting on the rock, putting my hand into the water, letting Matt hold me, how I was complete in his love. And I'd like to dive one more time for my gold. And oh, I forgot to tell you, I placed the three gold nuggets I took from the river in his pants pocket. He left for war with them, not knowing they were there. Bet he was startled to find them.

I do not wish for a funeral. I have said this in a letter to my friends. No crying. I will see my husband, my baby, and Mam. This will be joyful.

I heard the doctor say, "She's ready to go."

I heard a nurse weep.

So—I will run off now, skip on the road, down the hill.

Afterword

I just finished reading *Blown Apart*, and am deeply, deeply moved. Before I came to the computer I went back to page one and read ten or so pages; everything about the story's future is right there; amazing. The structure is neat and tightly woven. Impressive. Nothing extra or wasted.

I am affected in a deep personal way by the characters and their lives; I went through a lot of it, side by side, with Dawn. Many moments are close to moments in my life; old sadnesses were awakened, but with Mam's words being joined to them! Mam helped me, as well as Dawn. I SAW the scenes in my mind, have vivid images of place. I saw the river, the water, the story, the villagers, Dawn and Matt, naked under a bush, entwined. I was *there!*

I am left with sadness, at how the war took Dawn's life and shook it inside out or "blew it apart." It's a true feeling of sadness; Mam gone, so long ago, but at least there by her side through all of it; Pa, also gone, to return many years hence, perhaps broken, as he did not find another Mam. How could he? Mam was one of a kind; Mam was Mother personified, her wisdom a mantle to teach and protect her husband and her daughter; Mam was comfort, guidance into all things wide and deep, from being a growing girl to the entwining of past and present, to the immensity of the universe and Dawn's place in it, to hope and clarity, to acceptance of what is. I love Mam. More in Dawn's life was blown apart: Fred's departure, and with him, her dreams of life in the place she knew in her bones, how to live such a life, how to paint, do midwifery, survive. Then there was Matt, and this is where I feel especial sadness; that he pulled her in, where she could start to open herself to love (though she was not sure of her love), and then marriage and the baby; all of that gone, with the start of war.

I am left with a sense of despair about war, at its cruelty, though glad for the response of the little village, to remain One, strong and connected; that was beautiful. Left with a sense of sadness that the pre-WWII rural Maine life does not exist anymore. Left with a sense of wonder, at rural life, with all the magnificent details of daily life; these details touched me so; in 1968 I was married in Philadelphia, then came to Maine with my husband, and lived a sort-of old-fashioned life in Poland Spring; and then again, in 1992 when I moved to Phillips to teach at UMF, but lived as close as I could to a meaningful rural life. Margaret Brinton paints that old Maine life in a way that tells me she has known it, or at least, learned it, in the deep way that shows the fabric of the days and nights.

I love that Dawn learned to be independent from Mam; this carried her through life, once the war was over and done, and the people she loved, gone. Did she live life woodenly after that? Perhaps, at least somewhat. But with Mam ever by her side.

I believe all of the characters.

Dialogue is beautiful, especially Mam's words, and then the way those words come alive in Dawn's life.

The voice is consistent and real throughout; the voice has that strong sense of looking back over time, dipping in here and there to moments to be remembered. The voice is tender and loving, with a touch of sadness. Nothing trite, not a word. Words pierce me with their strength. The voice pulls present, past and future all together; occasionally I am unsure where I am, but I figure it out quickly.

Brinton blends narrative and dialogue and description beautifully, but I do feel this takes away some of the tension; just as the story moves forward, in dialogue, Dawn takes me back to Mam or some other aspect of that life. I believe this is the voice of the story, though. I didn't begin to feel tension until around page 115; from there, I could not read fast enough.

Elizabeth Cooke

English and Creative Writing Prof. Emeritus

University of Maine at Farmington

Margaret Brinton Collinson, born and raised outside Philadelphia, received her BFA in creative writing from the University of Maine at Farmington. She worked for a number of years as feature/news writer for the *Lewiston Sun Journal*, *Franklin Journal*, *Daily Bulldog*. She has taught creative writing to adult education classes, English composition at Central Maine Community College. She has studied abroad in Ireland (Drogheda Grammar School), Canada (Banff School of

Fine Arts, drama), and in Switzerland (Goetheanum School of the Arts). She lives with her husband, eight ducks, one cat, in Farmington, Maine.

www.ingramcontent.com/pod-product-compliance
Lightning Source LLC
Chambersburg PA
CBHW020644250626
47154CB00008B/2804